FORT VENGEANCE

Major Dan Fayes was sent to Fort Costain in Arizona to end the Apache reign of terror. The Apaches struck swiftly, armed with new Henry rifles. With his troop's survival hanging in the balance, Fayes suddenly discovered that one of his officers was a traitor. A man who would be riding at his back in the showdown battle . . .

GORDON D. SHIRREFFS

FORT VENGEANCE

Complete and Unabridged

LINFORD
Leicester

First published in the U.S.A. in 1957 by
Popular Library,
New York

First Linford Edition
published November 1986

British Library CIP Data

Shirreffs, Gordon D.
Fort vengeance.—Large print ed.—
Linford western library
I. Title
813′.54[F] PS3569.H/

ISBN 0-7089-6287-4

Published by
F. A. Thorpe (Publishing) Ltd.
Anstey, Leicestershire
Set by Rowland Phototypesetting Ltd.
Bury St. Edmunds, Suffolk
Printed and bound in Great Britain by
T. J. Press (Padstow) Ltd., Padstow, Cornwall

To My Mother, Rose

Foreword

FORT COSTAIN, Arizona Territory, was built on a branch of the lonely San Ignacio. Don't look for it on the maps, for the War Department ordered it abandoned in 1890. The site is near a rutted gravel road which cuts off from the state highway which closely follows the old Butterfield Trail. Follow the gravel road for twenty miles until you see the only outstanding feature of the terrain, a gaunt pinnacle of rock which thrusts itself up from the barren soil like a warning finger. Beyond this pinnacle is another rutted trail that leads to the mesa where Fort Costain once was. The rock is called Intchi-dijin Rock by the Apaches, or Black Wind Rock by the whites. It too has a story.

Scattered through the ocotillo, mesquite and prickly pear on the mesa top you can still see low mounds of adobe, the old buildings of the post. Shards of pink and blue glass litter the hard earth, mingled with old horseshoes, rusty metal and corroded brass buttons. It is all that is left of Fort Costain, once an isolated outpost of the United States Army.

The hills about Fort Costain are quiet now, brooding beneath the bright sunlight and the starlit nights. Civilization has passed it by, but history remembers it in the dusty files of the War Department and in the yellowed newspaper clippings of the early seventies. It was listed as Fort Costain by the War Department. To the men who served there it had another name . . . *Fort Vengeance*.

1

THE ABBOTT-DOWNING swayed easily on its great leather thoroughbraces; sideways as the spinning wheels hit the chuckholes; yellow dust flowed through the open windows and sifted between the cracks, coating everything inside.

Dan Fayes opened his eyes to look out at the hazy hills to the north. Somewhere in there was Fort Costain, his destination. The dust gritted between his teeth and abraded his throat, and he suddenly wanted the comfort and taste of a long nine. He slid his hand inside his coat, feeling for his cigar case. Then he looked at the young woman seated opposite him. Her scarf was tied across the lower part of her oval face. Her hazel eyes were steady, self-possessed.

She spoke through the fine scarf. "If you wish to smoke," she said, "please do. It can't be worse than this dust."

Dan smiled. "Thanks. The tobacco might cut the dust in my throat."

"I doubt it."

Dan took out a cigar and lit it. He snapped open the lid of his repeater watch. "Half after four. A long afternoon."

The big man seated beside the young woman looked up and nodded. "We'll be at Tres Cabezas home station within the hour."

Dan took his cigar from his mouth. "You know this country, Mister Manners?"

"I'm division inspector on this line."

"Tres Cabezas is my stop."

"Then you must be headed for Mesquite Wells?"

Dan shook his head. "Fort Costain."

The girl eyed Dan and then looked away.

Manners accepted a cigar from Dan. "You're army then?"

"Yes."

"I hope you're not assigned there, Fayes."

"How so?"

"Devilish place. Out on the devil's hind leg."

"I understand it isn't far from Mesquite Wells."

Manners laughed. "That isn't saying much. Begging your pardon, Miss Moore."

She looked at Manners. "No apology is necessary."

Dan leaned back. "You're from Mesquite Wells, Miss Moore?"

"I live near there with my father."

There was a veiled look of amusement in Manners' eyes. "There's no branch line to Mesquite Wells."

"I'll be picked up at Tres Cabezas," said Dan. "Perhaps you can ride with me, Miss Moore?"

"Thanks. We usually ride in army transportation from here to Mesquite Wells. My father does some contracting for Fort Costain."

The coach swayed around a curve. Manners pointed with his cigar. "Tres Cabezas."

Dan slid along the seat and looked through the billowing dust. A low rock structure showed on a knoll in front of a crescent-shaped area of rock. The hills were some miles north of the station. A triple-headed formation of rock showed dimly through the purple haze. Tres Cabezas. Three Heads. A damned lonely, forgotten speck of civilization on the Arizona landscape. Arizona hadn't changed much since his last tour of duty there in '59 and '60, thirteen years before.

Harriet Moore adjusted her scarf with a gloved hand. She studied the lean planes of Dan's face. The well-trimmed blond mustache with the faintest trace of red in it; the wideset gray eyes. He was army all right. "US" probably was branded on his lean cavalryman's flank. An officer, like all the others at Fort Costain, yet somehow different.

The driver snapped his twelve-foot lash and the six mules increased their pace. The greasy chuckle of the hubs rose in time to the steady clucking of the sandboxes.

Moore grinned. "Silver always comes into a station in style. Nobody to see him come in but hostlers and greaseboys, but he isn't one to miss a grand entry."

The coach swayed across a gravelly wash

and hit the far side. It came to a brake-shrieking halt in front of the station. "Ho, greasers!" yelled Silver.

The unkempt hostlers trotted out the relief team as the Mexican greaseboy slaked the hot axles. The shotgun messenger opened the coach door. "Tres Cabezas," he said.

Dan dropped to the ground after Miss Moore. He winced as his left leg came back to life. Unless he kept moving the Minié ball wound stiffened a little. He took his gun case from the coach. Manners said, "I owe you a drink for the cigar," and sauntered toward the station.

Miss Moore drew the scarf from her face. She would have been classed as a little better than plain in the fashionable society of New York or Washington. In Arizona Territory, still a man's world in '73, she caught every male eye.

"I'll enjoy your company to Mesquite Wells," said Dan. "Perhaps you'll tell me about the country?"

"There isn't much to tell. The mines are dying out. Cattlemen are trying to get a foothold. Most of the Apaches are uncomfortable on their reservations. Some of the *broncos* try to incite the reservation bucks into going to war."

They passed the thick, bolt-studded door and entered the big low common room. A zinc-topped bar stretched along one wall. A lanky trooper leaned against it, holding a whisky glass in his hand. He glanced casually at Dan and with interest at Harriet. "Hello, Harriet," he said.

She smiled. "Corporal Tanner! What are you doing here?"

He grinned. "I wish I had come to meet you. I'm lookin' for Sergeant Haley."

"Why?"

He downed his drink. "Old Mike went over the hill last week."

"I don't believe it!"

Tanner shrugged. "You can take my word for it. Old Mike got a bellyful of Fort Costain. We've had four desertions so far this month. Twenty-two since the first of the year. Two suicides. It's worse than when you were last here, Harriet. Maybe you ought to marry me and leave here. My old man says I can have his farm in Iowa."

"What about that girl in Tucson, Bob?"

Tanner grinned. "You think I'd look at *her* if you was to let me court *you*?"

Manners went behind the bar and got a bottle and glasses. "Come on, Fayes," he said.

Dan eyed the bottle. *Surely one or two wouldn't hurt.*

Manners filled the glasses, eying Harriet as she passed into the hallway. "Nice filly. Too damned bad about her."

Tanner turned slowly. "What was that you said?"

"Too damned bad about her."

Tanner hitched up his trousers. He was slightly drunk. "You watch what you say! You hear?"

Manners smiled. "No offense, Corporal. What I meant was that it's too bad she has to stay at her father's place."

Dan took his glass. "Where's that?"

Manners relit his cigar. "Jim Moore has the hog ranch on the road between Mesquite Wells and Fort Costain, just over the post boundary line. Saloon. General store. Freight yard. Unofficial officers' club."

"Harriet is a lady," said Tanner.

Manners eyed him. "I didn't say she wasn't."

Dan sipped his liquor. The fire of it swept through him. The same old spark that usually ignited a roaring holocaust in him. It was his first drink since the interview with General Sherman in Washington. He had broken his promise.

Manners downed a second drink. "Well, I'll be on my way. As it is, it'll be after dark when we reach Calabasas swing station. I'll see you, Fayes."

Tanner eyed Dan. "You headin' for Mesquite Wells?"

"Fort Costain."

Tanner's reddened eyes narrowed. "You ain't no fresh fish," he said. "You an officer?"

"Yes. Major Fayes."

Tanner straightened up a little. "I'm sorry, sir. I was just cuttin' the dust."

Benny wiped the zinc. "I coulda told you he was an officer, Tanner."

Dan hesitated. The noncom was on duty, tracking down a deserter, and therefore should have left the forty-rod strictly alone. Still, Dan had not officially taken over command of his new post. He removed his cigar from his mouth. "I'd go easy, Corporal," he said.

"Yes, sir."

"Where's my room?" asked Dan of the bartender.

"Down the hallway. Last one on the right. Ain't fancy, but we don't often get stopovers here."

Dan picked up his luggage and went out. He heard Tanner's unsteady voice behind him at the bar: "After he's at Costain for awhile he won't worry none abut me havin' a few drinks. Not after he sees how them *officers* swill day in and day out."

Dan continued down the corridor to the room at the end. He dumped his luggage and dropped on the dusty cot. The liquor was working within him as it always did.

Dan puffed at his cigar. This was his last chance to stay in the service. The Benzine Board was lopping off excess and inefficient officers right and left, stripping high rankers from the shrinking Regular Army. The Congressional appropriation of 1869 had cut down the regular infantry regiments from forty-five to twenty-five. The cavalry had been increased for frontier duty, and many first-class doughboy officers had transferred to the mounted arm.

The words of General Cump Sherman seemed to come to Dan on the desert wind. "You're about due for the Benzine Board, Fayes. Your record was spotless. You were a colonel of volunteers at twenty-three. But since Appomattox, it has been one continuous round of drinking, women and gambling while on your inspection tours. Luckily you still have many friends in the service. They have prevailed on me to give you another chance. I'm assigning you to Fort Costain, Arizona Territory. It's a rotten mess. Don't thank me, Dan. Your results will save, or *lose*, your commission. If you fail . . . well . . . send in your resignation before you get your orders to appear before the Benzine Board. It will be easier on all of us."

Dan closed his eyes. The damned insatiable craving for liquor had started the last year of the war. Before that time he had had his share of bottle courage, but then it had been a war of movement. The fighting at Spotsylvania Court House, in the Mule Shoe area, had shifted the balance from a love of action and excitement to that of a matter of holding on to the last shreds of courage for decency's sake.

Fighting with his regiment, part of the battlewise Sixth Corps, he had been struck in the left thigh by a Minié ball. The hours that had followed, lying in a rain-filled ditch, tinted red by flowing blood, listening to the groans and shrieks of the wounded, had somehow cracked the citadel walls of his inner spirit. That rainy night a nameless enemy had gained control. From then on, through the remainder of the war, he had leaned heavily on the glass crutch.

The bottle had been his aid and comfort when his leg ached intolerably, and when the wartime memories came back to gibber and drool at him in the night. He had requested a transfer back to the cavalry, his original arm, after Appomattox, pleading the wound which made it difficult to march. Surprisingly enough he had been dropped no lower than major, with duty as a cavalry inspector. Slowly but steadily liquor had saddled him and tightened the cinch. Then it had slipped a spade bit into his mouth to make its control of him complete and sure.

Dan's duties had carried him from the Texas-Mexican border, where yellowlegs had watched the ambitions of Maximilian, through the Indian Territory up to Forts Laramie, Fetterman and Kearney, then down through Colorado and New Mexico to Forts Union, Craig and Bliss. Liquor flowed like water at post affairs. Old comrades from West Point and the war helped him along his wet road. Then there were the nights spent in raw frontier towns where there was no amusement except hurdy-gurdy girls and saloons.

Dan opened his eyes and watched a centipede crawl across the window sill. *Had it really been eight years?* He had spent the last year in Washington, preparing reports and recommendations, bidding farewell to discharged officers who had served their country in time of war and peace and who now had been callously thrown back into the mad civilian struggle for money, most of them by training ill-equipped for the fight. Over seven hundred and fifty of them had been cast adrift.

Dan dozed uneasily for a time and then got up to wash. The sun had died and he lit a candle lantern. He eyed himself critically in the cracked mirror. The gray eyes were darkly shadowed. The reddish-blond hair had lost the shine of youth. His hard hands gripped the sides of the washstand. This time he had to make good. He would never be able to face himself in a mirror again if he didn't. It had always been his dream to end his life in service harness. If he failed he might as well be dead; for a man without a dream was truly dead.

2

THE common room was lit by a big hanging Rochester harp lamp. The yellow pool of light flooded the table set with chipped graniteware for two. The greasy odor of cooking filled the station. Miss Moore was already seated, still wearing her gray traveling costume. Benny bustled into the room from the kitchen bearing a loaded tray. "Mex strawberries, sowbelly and jamoke," he said apologetically. "Our fresh supplies ain't come in yet."

Corporal Tanner was nowhere in sight. "We'll be dining alone," said Harriet.

"Quite cozy," said Dan.

"You've been west before this time?"

"My first assignment was as a shavetail at old Fort Buchanan near Sonoita Creek."

"That is now Fort Crittenden."

"Then I served at Fort Grant at the base of the Pinalenos most of the time."

"So you know the Apache?"

Her tone caused Dan to look up quickly. "Yes. Why do you ask?"

"Last year there was a great deal of trouble in the Tonto Basin."

"I understood the Apaches in this area were living quietly on their reservations."

She raised her head. "They've never really been quiet. The Tucson Ring has been working overtime to stir them up."

"The Tucson Ring?"

She nodded. "Grafters, rustlers, dishonest contractors and frontier riffraff. Their plan is to keep the Apaches restless so that the War Department will be forced to keep troops here. Crooked politicians and contractors cheat the government on hay, lumber and other supplies. The settlements near the posts profit from the soldier trade."

"You seem to be well informed, Miss Moore."

She nodded. "I've heard my father and his business friends speak of it many times."

"Has your father been long in business out here?"

She flushed a little. "Since after the war. He was with Carleton's California Column in 1862 when it came through here. Later he was stationed at Fort Bowie in Apache Pass. He took his discharge out here and sent for me after my mother died."

"Do you like living near Mesquite Wells?" The instant he saw the look in her eyes Dan regretted his question.

"As long as you are going to Fort Costain, Major Fayes, you might as well know the truth. My father runs a combination general store and saloon with a small freighting business as well. The place is known far and wide as Moore's Hog Ranch."

"Running a saloon is no dishonor, Miss Moore, as long as it is run with decency."

She stood up. "To *some* people it is a dishonor. People who do not have my father's decency." She left the common room and walked outside.

Dan finished his meal and followed her. She stood by the high-walled corral watching the fine paring of the moon as it rose above the eastern heights. The light sharply accentuated the angular peaks.

"There is nothing more beautiful than the desert at night," he said.

She nodded. "I'm glad you said that. So many officers think otherwise."

"May I smoke?"

"I like the odor of good tobacco." She turned and leaned back against the wall. "Smoking must be a great solace."

He lit up, the flare of the lucifer showing his lean tanned face. "It is."

"I often wonder if women would be accepted in society if they took up smoking."

"Not cigars, I hope."

She laughed. "No."

The moon rose higher, flooding the desert with silvery light, marking the desert growths with sharp shadows. "Are you a brevet major?" she asked.

"No."

She eyed him. "Then you will be relieving Captain Ellis Morgan. He's CO of A Company. Costain is a three-company post, you know."

He nodded. "How long has Morgan been in command?"

"Three months. He succeeded Major Dunphy."

"What happened to Dunphy?"

She seemed surprised. "You don't know? Of course you wouldn't. It was hushed up." She became curiously quiet.

"I'd like to know," he said. "You might as well tell me. I'll find out when I get there in any case."

"Yes," she said quietly. She turned and placed her slim hands behind her back. "Jim drank a great deal. It had a terrible hold on him. His officers and men laughed behind his back. It didn't help Jim any. *He knew*. There was a terrible fear in him. He had a fine war record under Wilson." She looked away. "But the guerrilla warfare of the Apaches was too much for him. He sought his courage in the bottle. Apparently he didn't find enough there. One night he shot himself."

Dan took his cigar from his mouth. Her words had struck home like the smash of the Minié ball which had wounded him. "You seem to know a lot about Jim Dunphy," he said quietly.

Her steady eyes held his. "Yes. You see . . . we were engaged to be married."

In the silence that followed a coyote gave tongue out in the wastes.

Dan relit his cigar. "I'm sorry I talked you into telling me about it."

She shrugged. "You would have found out. Don't condemn Jim too harshly. Some men follow a walk of life for which they are fitted. Others try to follow a way of life for which they are *not* fitted, yet lack the courage to leave it. Jim was one of those. There was too much pride in him to let him resign."

"It isn't an easy thing to do, Miss Moore."

"Perhaps there are times when it takes more courage to turn back than to go ahead."

He touched the puckered bullethole beneath the left trouser leg. In that last bloody charge at the Mule Shoe he had been afraid. Other officers had turned back, with fear etched on their white faces, but Dan had gone on into the leaden sleet, rallying his men. He had paid the price. A far greater price than an occasional twinge in his left leg.

She paced back and forth. "Dad sent me to Albuquerque to stay with his sister after Jim died. For a long time I did not want to come back and then I knew I had to."

"Why are you confiding in me, Miss Moore?"

She stopped and looked up into his shadowy face. "I don't really know. Perhaps because you are going to take Jim's place. Good night, Major Fayes." She turned and walked quickly into the station.

Dan loosened his collar and let the dry desert wind seep down beneath his shirt. The light went on in her room, the next one to his. His secret had always been his own. It wasn't any longer. She knew.

The cold rain slanted down, pudding in the greasy mud of the tangled woods about Spotsylvania Courthouse. The leaves dripped and the pools of lead-colored water were dimpled by the drops. Dead and wounded of both sides were scattered thickly, half-sunken in the mud. There was a steady groaning, almost inhuman in sound, broken now and then by an agonized scream. A foul smell hung in the wet air. A miasma of blood, powder smoke, sour clothing and death.

The rain was fine and steady, now and then illuminated by ghostly fingers of lightning. A dead man lay five feet from Dan, his twisted fingers gripping his bloody undershirt. A muddy footprint showed on his bluish face. Somewhere in the night a Union band played a polka, more like a dirge in the saturated darkness. The last of the staggering, wild-eyed Union assault troops had long disappeared into the night, leaving a bloody debris of dead and wounded to mark their attack.

The wind swept through the dripping woods, bowing the trees like the heads of keening women. A figure moved through the soaked brush, bending now and then over a body. The man knelt beside a young Union officer. A flash of lightning showed the gleam of the knife and the severed finger in the man's hand, with a ring still on it. The ghoul wore Union blue.

Dan shifted, feeling for his Colt. It was gone, lost in the thick mud. His sword lay shattered at his feet. Dan rolled to one side, gritting his teeth at the spasm of pain which shot through his shattered left leg. He felt in his pocket, drawing out a stubby Southern swivel-barreled derringer, souvenir of Antietam. He cocked it, hoping to God it was not too wet to fire.

The ghoul came close. He stopped at Dan's feet and then reached out with a muddy hand. Dan fired up at the dim face. The lightning flashed, revealing the jagged cut of the mouth as the soft slug smashed home under the bearded chin. The ghoul pitched forward across Dan's body. Warm blood dripped down on Dan's face.

Muskets popped from the shattered Rebel breastworks as the shot alerted the defenders. The limp body jerked as the slugs drove home in it. More blood ran down on Dan's face. He screamed as it blinded him. Again and again.

Dan sat bolt upright. Cold sweat soaked his undershirt. He smashed his back against the adobe wall behind him, clawing for his service forty-five. Then sanity came slowly back to him. He saw the white-plastered walls of the little room and the dappled moonlight on his bed.

Dan's hands shook as he wiped the sweat from his face. It had been almost a year since he had had that particular nightmare. He dropped his legs over the side of the bed and held his face in his hands. What was it Harriet Moore had said? *Perhaps it takes more courage to go back than to go ahead.*

3

THE morning wind scrabbled at the thick walls of the station. A crissal thrasher gave voice somewhere out in the mesquite. Dan opened his eyes. After his nightmare he had lain awake for hours, wishing for a drink. Now he arose and splashed water on his face and dressed swiftly. Out on the sunlit desert, a thread of smoke floated up from a distant peak, raveled by the fresh wind. Dan swung his gunbelt about his lean hips and settled it. He slipped a double-barreled derringer into his coat pocket. At the bottom of one of his bags was the little swivel-barreled derringer he had found at Antietam. He never saw it without thinking of that rain-soaked night at the Mule Shoe, yet he could not bring himself to get rid of it.

Harriet Moore was at the table when he entered the common room. She smiled. "Good morning. You slept well?"

"Yes," he lied.

The steady hazel eyes held his for a moment and then she looked away. Dan sat down and filled a cup with steaming black coffee. He wondered if she had heard him during the night.

Benny entered the room. "Mush and sowbelly. The hens ain't layin' this mornin'," he said with a grin.

While they ate they heard the popping of a whip out in the desert, followed by the steady thud of hoofs and the rolling of swift wheels. A hostler looked in through the doorway. "The Dougherty from Fort Costain is here," he called out.

The vehicle ground to a halt outside of the station. A dusty trooper entered the room. "Major Fayes here?" he asked.

Dan stood up. "Yes."

"Trooper Samuel Booth. Dougherty driver."

"My luggage is in the end room. Bring Miss Moore's as well from the room next to it."

"Yes, sir." Booth glanced at Harriet. His homely face broke into a grin. "Miss

Harriet! I heard you was coming home."
"I arrived last night, Sam."
"Your Paw will sure be tickled."
Dan paid the tab and went outside, lighting a cigar. He walked toward the Dougherty. A civilian leaned against it, his face shaded by a battered Kossuth hat. He gave Dan a sketchy salute. "Gila Barnes," he said, "government scout."
"Major Fayes."
"You don't remember me?"
"By God!" said Dan, "you were at Fort Grant with me in '60!"
Barnes grinned. "Yeh. You was a shavetail then. Nantan Eclatten."
Dan laughed as he recalled the name given to him by friendly Pinalenos. Nantan Eclatten. Raw Virgin Lieutenant. The name had persisted even after rough fighting against the elusive Intchi-dijin, Black Wind, a pure quill *bronco* of the Tontos. Dan gripped the scout's hard hand. "I'd have thought that by now you would have been long gone to the House of Spirits."
Barnes shifted his chew of spit-or-drown.

"Oh, they tried a few times. My mother always said I'd come to no good."

Dan looked past the scout at the thin tendril of smoke against the clear sky. "Did you see that smoke, Gila?"

Gila nodded. He spat accurately at a gecko lizard, splattering the fine scales with brown juice. "We been seein' 'em for three days."

"What's up?"

"Only smoke so far." Gila wiped his stained beard. "Don't yuh remember, Dan?"

Dan grinned. "Sudden puff means strange party on plains below. Rapid puffs means travelers well armed and numerous. Steady smoke for some time means to collect scattered bands at some predesignated point with hostile intention if practicable. What's going on, Gila?"

"*Quien sabe?* The Tontos have been restless but haven't broken loose. The Pinalenos are at peace."

"So?"

"The Chiricahuas may be up this far. Might even be a band of White Mountain

'Paches, or wandering Mimbrenos from New Mexico."

"The road is safe?"

Gila shrugged. "Few roads in Arizona are ever really safe. We left the fort last night and camped out at Yellow Wash. Nothin' happened."

Harriet came from the station followed by Booth carrying the luggage. "Hello, Gila," she said with a smile, holding out her hand.

Gila wiped his hand on his greasy shirt. His craggy face broke into a wide grin. "Miss Harriet! Well, I'll be damned! Tickles me pink to see yuh."

"Is everything all right at the ranch?"

"Fair to middlin'. Your Paw is fine. Arm bothers him onct in a while. Outside of that he's as healthy as a cub bear."

Booth rolled up the canvas boot cover and stowed away the luggage. Dan placed his cased rifle in the wagon. Gila helped the young woman in. Booth climbed into the driver's seat and took the ribbons. "All right, sir?" he asked.

"Roll it, Booth."

Booth slapped the reins on the dusty rumps of the wheel mules. The Dougherty rolled out onto the stage road and then turned onto the yellow ribbon of rutted track which trended north toward the low hills. The smoke was gone now.

The sun climbed higher, soaking the desert in yellow heat. The dust rose from hoofs and wheels. The ragged hills, bleached as white in places as dead men's bones, were stippled with brush. A dull haze was forming over the mountains. It was a dead land with the slender shoots of ocotillo showing above the high mescal plants. Chollas spread their fangs among beds of prickly pear. A lone saguaro raised long arms in supplication to the pitiless sky.

"Like traveling on the moon," said Dan to himself. Harriet turned. "That's the first thing you've said since we left Tres Cabezas."

Dan leaned back on the hard jump seat. "Silence always seems to be a part of the desert. It seems almost unholy to speak too loud."

"As in a church."

"In a way."

"Some church," said Gila over his shoulder. He slowly cut a fresh chew of spit-or-drown. "I always think of the desert like it was a cougar. Nice to look at, when you're at a distance. Close up you get the truth. The claws inside the velvet."

"You sound like a poet, Gila," said Harriet. "You've been reading again."

Gila stood the chew into his mouth and spoke thickly. "Oh, I didn't read that. A shavetail onct said that to me years ago when we both got lost out here. No water. No trail."

Dan eyed Gila. "I remember," he said quietly.

Gila nodded. "It was you."

"Only I didn't say the desert was like a cougar. I said it was like a woman."

Gila turned. "Waal, I didn't want to say that in front of Harriet, Dan."

Harriet eyed Dan. "That sounds bitter."

He looked out across the harsh desert. "It was meant to be. At that time anyway."

"And now?"

He looked at her. "I'm not so sure it still isn't the truth."

She leaned back and studied the lean planes of his face. She had struck a responsive chord in him. A strange man. It *must* have been him screaming in the night.

Gila suddenly jerked his head, and held up a hand.

Booth reined the team to a dusty halt. Dan looked out of a side window. High in the brassy sky was a drifting spot, like a scrap of charred paper. A revulsion formed in him. A buzzard.

Gila rubbed his corded neck. Then he slid from his seat and drew his long-barreled Spencer rifle from the wagon. "I'll be right back," he said.

Dan jumped from the wagon. "Wait," he said. He stripped the case from his new Winchester.

Gila whistled as he saw the fine weapon. "What is it? Rimfire?"

"Model 73. Brand-new. Caliber .44. Centerfire. More wallop than the old Model 66 rimfire."

Gila padded off through the brush with

Dan close behind. "What is it, Gila?"

"We'll see in a minute. Didn't yuh see them hoss tracks in the soft sand near the road?"

"No."

"Get the crust offin them eyeballs! You're back in Apacheria, Danny."

Gila stopped in a clearing and eyed some horse droppings. He smashed them with his rifle butt. "Cavalry hoss. Oats in the droppings. Dropped last night, I'd say." His eyes studied the harsh earth like a page in a book. "Hoss walking slow."

They went on. Gila held up a hand. A crumpled figure lay half-concealed beneath a mesquite clump. The half-inch yellow stripe showed on the blue trousers. "Come on," said Gila.

Dan levered a round into the chamber.

Gila rolled the body over. Dan looked into the bloody face of Corporal Tanner. The scalp had been cut neatly from the elongated skull. The jowls had loosened like wet pie dough. Flies rose in a buzzing cloud from the clotted red abomination of the naked skull. The mouth gaped open revealing the stained teeth. Gila spat deliberately. He pointed at the side of the skull, smashed like an egg. "They made damned sure his spirit wouldn't follow them for vengeance."

"Why a scalping? That usually isn't Apache practice."

Gila shook his head. The faded eyes held Dan's. "Not unless they plan a scalp dance."

Gila walked about. "Welcome back to Arizona, Dan," he said. "There's a blanket in the wagon. We'd better wrap him up so's Harriet don't see him."

The sun glinted on glass. Dan picked up an empty rye bottle. "When did it happen, Gila?"

Gila squatted by the corpse. "'Bout dawn, I'd say."

"Tontos?"

"*Quien sabe?* Tontos. Pinalenos. Mimbrenos. White Mountain, Chiricahuas."

"Much of this going on?"

Gila shook his head. "Onct in awhile we find a dead man in the hills. Ain't no way of tellin' who did the job."

Dan eyed the brooding hills. "You think we're safe?"

"The pass is wide. Not much cover. We got three good rifles and know how to use 'em. Harriet can shoot for record if she has to."

"Why in God's name didn't you bring an escort?"

"There hasn't been that much trouble. Besides, Cap'n Morgan said he couldn't spare the men."

"I don't like it."

Gila stood up. "Take it easy, Dan. This loco bastard musta been drunk when he reached here. Mebbe passed out in the saddle. Hoss walks offn the road. *Somebody* sees a chanct to get a good rifle, pistol and hoss. Temptin' it was. They watches Tanner. Drops him. *Yah-ik-te.* He is not present; he is wanting."

"Why would they scalp him? It's a dead giveaway."

It was a strange face that turned toward Dan. "I've done a little myself, Dan. Wore Navajo hair on my leggins while scoutin' for Kit Carson's First New Mexico. I wasn't the only one. Somebody's brewin' medicine, Dan. *Big* medicine."

Dan went back to the wagon and had Booth unhitch a mule while he got a blanket. He did not look at Harriet. He rode the mule back to Gila, who was coming out of the brush. "They was three of them. One ridin' a mare. Three hosses was in the brush. Four hosses rides off. One of them without a rider."

The mule shied and blowed as they placed the blanketed form across his back. Gila opened his hand and showed Dan a brass cartridge case.

"So?"

"Forty-four Henry rimfire. One shot. Not many repeaters in 'Pache hands around here."

"That doesn't mean much."

"Mebbe. Mebbe not." Gila dropped the hull into his pocket. "Looks like I got to get off my dead rump at Fort Costain and take a look-see into them hills when we get back."

They led the mule back through the brush. Now and then Dan looked back over his shoulder. The desert was as silent as Corporal Tanner's grave would be.

The Dougherty bounced and swayed across the rough ground, sinking now into a deep sun-baked rut, and then bouncing out of it. Now and then Dan glanced back at the still, blanketed form in the rear of the vehicle, but most of the time he scanned the low hills on either side of the quiet pass. As Gila had said, the pass was wide, without too much cover. Gila rode with his long Spencer butted on the floorboards, leaning on the weapon, eying the hills from beneath the sloppy brim of his Kossuth hat.

Harriet held Dan's forty-five in her lap. Her face was pale, but she had not gone into hysterics at the sight of the body. She was steady. Afraid of course, but steady. There was a difference.

They rounded a sharp turn and Gila looked at Dan. "We can turn off soon onto the fort road. Or do you want to take Harriet to her father first?"

"The ranch, Gila."

"Keno."

Dan slanted back his hat and looked toward the hills. A gaunt pinnacle of rock thrust itself up from the barren soil like a warning finger. Then Dan saw the strange figure seated in a hollow of the pinnacle, almost as though sitting in a comfortable armchair. Thin arms hung across the bony knees which protruded from beneath a greasy buckskin kilt. Loose moccasins hung about the skinny calves. The button-toed, thigh-length, hard-soled desert footwear of the Apache. The *n'deh b'keh*.

Booth reined in swiftly and scrabbled for his issue trapdoor Springfield carbine.

Gila raised his head. "Looks like a damned mummy."

The four whites looked up the slope at the motionless seated figure. The Apache was old. His hair was dirty gray, bound by a calico headband. His ragged huck shirt hung open exposing his gaunt chest, the ribs protruding like ridges of granite through brown sand. He did not move.

"Is he dead?" asked Harriet softly.

"No," said Dan. The Apache was no more than fifty feet from the motionless wagon, as though graven from the very rock on which he sat. There was an uncanny stillness in the hot air. Even the mules stopped their small movements.

The Apache moved, raising a skinny arm. He spoke slowly in good Spanish. The voice was firm and clear as though a young man spoke. "Do not be afraid. None of the young men are here. Only I, who am old beyond belief, and harmless to you."

"What is it you want?" asked Dan in his rusty Spanish.

"I know you, Nantan Eclatten!"

An icy finger seemed to trace the length of Dan's spine. "No."

"We have fought against each other in years past. In the old days, before the great war of the White-eyes. You have been gone a long time."

"I do not remember, old man."

The Apache lowered his skinny arm. "Then, Nantan Eclatten, there is no respect in you for an old enemy? Was I not a good warrior? Did I not strike terror into you as you did to me when we fought?"

Dan shifted in his seat, moving his rifle.

He had fought most of them before the war. Tontos, Pinalenos, Aravaipas and Chiricahuas.

"You do not remember Intchi-dijin?"

"Jesus!" said Gila. "Black Wind! I thought the old raider was long dead!"

Black Wind moved, and the sun glinted on a brass plate which hung from a thong about his withered neck. "Nantan Eclatten, in the old days you were but a boy, fit only to herd horses, and wear the head-scratching stick of the untried brave."

"Thanks," said Dan dryly.

"It is said that now you are a tried warrior. A chief wise in the ways of the white man's war. Why is it you come? Do the White-eyes plan vengeance on The People? Will there be war in this country again?"

"We are at peace with The People. But we have just found the body of one of our men. Scalped. Not five miles from here. Is this the doing of The People? If so, then it is *you* who plans war."

Black Wind raised his head a little. "You are sure it was done by my people?"

"Yes. There has been smoke in the skies.

Do you not have a treaty for peace with us?"

"Lies! Scraps of paper are covered with marks which have no meaning to The People. We are forced to make our marks on them. It says one thing. The White-eyed chiefs do another."

"*I* have signed no paper, Black Wind."

"It does not matter. Your people are not like mine. Each warrior has his say before he goes to war. Amongst your people a warrior does as he is told. You will go to war. There will be bloodshed."

"These are the words of a bitter old man."

"Listen, Nantan Eclatten! My people are angry. The young men sharpen their arrows and grease their guns. They buy fine rifles with the yellow iron which the White-eyes love more than anything else. They have asked my council and I have spoken. I advised peace, but if they do not heed my words your lodges will go up in smoke. Your wagons will be captured. Those of you who wear the blue suits will die in the mountains and deserts. The signal smokes will rise from here to Sonora."

"What is it they want, Old One?"

"Peace! But more than that! *Justice*! There is to be a meeting between the people and mine at San Ignacio Creek. It will end the same way!" Black Wind jerked the brass plate from the thong and held it out in a dirty claw. "This is the badge of betrayal! The reservation number given to a great chief as though he was one of your cows, sheep or goats! Am *I* to be only a number? I fled your reservation years ago, but I kept this badge of shame! Take it! Keep it! Remember it! For you shall not rest by day or night!" He hurled the plate into the roadway. It tinkled into a baked rut.

Dan felt cold sweat run down his sides.

Black Wind pointed a finger at the wagon. "There will come a time when you shall want to speak with me. Use that plate to pass through my warriors, before you choose the way of your dying! Farewell, Nantan Eclatten!"

The four whites looked down at the brass plate. When they raised their eyes again the ancient was gone, as though he had disappeared into the living rock itself.

Gila slid from the wagon and picked up the plate. He read it: "Black Wind. Number One. San Ignacio Reservation." Gila tossed the plate up and down in his hand. "I thought the old coot was long dead. He hasn't been seen around for years. He was the greatest of them all. A chosen son of Stenatliha. Knew every waterhole and rimrock trail from the Mogollons down to Durango. No living man, white or red, knows this country like he does. It's a damned good thing he's as old as he is."

"I'm not so sure about that."

Their eyes met. "Somehow I'm glad you're back, Dan," said Gila, "providin' you remember how to mix with 'Paches, and don't let your years in the war make you think you know everything about fighting."

"I won't."

There had been an eeriness about the whole episode. The pass brooded in the hot sun. Harriet's face was tense as she looked at the pinnacle of rock. "He knew you."

"It's possible. I remember now fighting against a chief called Black Wind. He was an old man even then."

"Yes." Her face was strange. "But what you don't know is that Black Wind *has been blind for over five years!*"

Gila handed the greasy plate to Dan. "Yes. I remember now."

Booth nervously rubbed his jaw. "Let's get out of here!"

The Dougherty rolled forward. Dan fingered the brass plate. A feeling of foreboding surged over him. The rock was empty of life. Black Wind's Rock.

4

MOORE'S RANCH was situated on a rocky hill overlooking the Mesquite Wells road. The walls were immensely thick, buttressed, pierced with narrow windows fitted with heavy metal shutters. The low roof was surrounded by a crenelated parapet. Beyond the house were high-walled corrals from which issued the bawling of mules. Heavy freight wagons stood near a field-rock warehouse. Outbuildings formed a quadrangle from which loopholes covered every foot of approach to the ranch.

Dan eyed the solid buildings. "Looks like a fort," he observed.

"It is," said Gila. "Jim built here right after the war. That was before Fort Costain's time. There was many a bloody wrangle around here before the 'Paches figgered the ranch was too tough a nut to crack."

Booth reined in the team near the main building. Dan helped Harriet down. She handed him his Colt. "Thanks. I'm glad I didn't have to use it."

"You might yet," said Booth gloomily.

Gila opened the thick door and they entered a huge pillared room. The floor was sand-strewn. Battered tables covered the floor. A long bar stretched along one wall. Shafts of sunlight peered through the narrow windows. A solidly built man hurried from behind the bar. "Harriet!" he said. "It's been a long time."

Harriet ran to him, and he drew her close with his left arm. The right sleeve was knotted just below the elbow. Jim Moore's face was seamed and furrowed; the face of a man who had spent most of his life outdoors in hard country. Harriet turned. "This is Major Fayes, Dad."

Moore held out his left hand. "The new CO of Fort Costain? Welcome, sir. The bar is open. I'd like to buy you a drink."

Dan shook his head. Booth wet his lips. Moore looked at the driver. "Is it all right if I buy Sam and Gila one?"

"Why not?"

Moore walked behind the bar. "Any trouble?"

Gila nodded. "Bob Tanner's tack is drove."

Moore turned quickly. "How so?"

"We found his body five miles the far side of the pass. Scalped."

Moore looked at Harriet and turned pale beneath the tan. "My God," he said, "I thought it was quiet."

"It ain't. We seen old Black Wind. He's hot under his stinkin' shirt. Claims his people are ready for war. Fact is, they ain't nothin' but a few rimrock *broncos* on the loose. Leastways, that's all that's been seen the last few months."

Moore nodded. "A commissioner is coming here one of these days for a conference at San Ignacio Creek." He downed a drink and eyed Dan. "I heard this morning that Hair Rope was seen near there with some of his *broncos*. He's pure quill, Major."

Gila refilled his glass. "Any of them carryin' Henry repeaters?"

Moore's eyes narrowed. "Damned if I know. Why?"

"Tanner was killed by one."

"That doesn't mean anything."

"Mebbe. Mebbe not. I've heard tell they'll pay up to two hundred in raw gold for one."

"You've been eating peyote."

"No. Last month three troopers went over the hill. One of them stole Capn' Morgan's Henry rifle. I met him in Tucson. The drunken bum told me Hair Rope bought all three Colts and Springfields from him and his mates for one hundred and fifty apiece in gold dust. Two hundred for the Henry."

Moore refilled the glasses. "Can you blame the troopers? Even white men will pay good money for those weapons rather than try to collect twenty dollars for turning in a deserter."

Dan eyed the ranch owner. "Seems as though some of the whites out here are as much against the army as the Apaches, Moore."

Moore placed his one hand flat on the

bar. "Not *all* of them, Major Fayes. Sure, we've got renegades, grafters and profiteers raising hell, but many of us are loyal citizens."

"Those people can raise hell out here."

"I'll agree to that. But as long as you have law officers, corrupt Indian Agents, yes, and even territorial and government politicians getting their cut, you're going to see a lot more of it." Moore turned to Gila. "You said Tanner was scalped."

"I did."

Moore rubbed his jaw. "Damned odd."

"That ain't all. Black Wind remembered Major Fayes here, and the old coot is stone-blind."

Booth nodded. "Puts the fear of God into a man sitting there and seein' that old bag of bones lookin' at you, knowin' damned well he can't see you, and yet talkin' as though his eyes was as good as they ever was."

Moore waved his hand. "There's some explanation. He might have had someone with him."

"By God, he didn't, Jim!" said Booth.

"It still figures. How many times have

you been shot at by Apaches without seeing them?"

Booth ran a finger inside his collar. "Too damned many!"

Jim nodded. "Black Wind got word that the command was changing at Fort Costain. He was wise that the major left Tres Cabezas. So the old goat sits in the sun like a Chinese idol and makes like a man that can see."

Dan took out a cigar. "It's possible."

Moore nodded. "Of course it is. I've seen some of these Apache medicinemen, the *diyis*, do some incredible stuff. Incredible until you analyzed it."

"We'd better get to the post," said Dan.

Moore reached for a bottle. "Compliments of the ranch, Major Fayes. Rye or bourbon? Perhaps you'd prefer *aguardiente* or good Baconora mezcal?"

Dan was about to refuse. "Mezcal," he said.

Moore placed the squat bottle on the bar.

"Thanks," said Dan. He turned to Harriet. "It was a great pleasure traveling with you, Miss Moore."

"Thank you," she said.

"I'm only sorry we found Corporal Tanner on the way."

"She's seen dead men before, Major Fayes," said Moore quietly.

Dan walked to the door and got into the Dougherty. Booth poured a quick drink and slopped it down, wiping his loose mouth. Gila grinned. They went out to the wagon.

Moore and Harriet stood at the door and watched the Dougherty roll down to the road. He looked at his daughter. "You've gotten over Jim Dunphy?" he asked softly.

"I think so."

Jim Moore leaned against the doorway. "When?"

She looked at him. "Why do you ask?"

Moore looked at the wagon. "Him."

She shrugged. "Another officer. They seem to come from the same mold."

"Not this one, Harriet."

"How do you know, Dad?"

He placed his arm about her slim waist. "Men have always been my business. Soldiers. Teamsters. Gamblers. Drunks. All the types and variations that make up the men of the frontier. Jim Dunphy was weak. Oh, he was a nice fellow. Many of the weak ones are."

She looked at the wagon. "And you think he's weak too?"

He laughed bitterly. "We all are. In this country a man's weaknesses show up better than most places. I wonder what his are? Women? Gambling? Liquor?"

"The unholy trio."

He nodded. "Yet there is something about him that *is* different."

"Why are you telling me this?"

He drew her close. "There was a way you looked at him. You've a great deal of your mother in you, Harriet."

"Is that bad?"

He shook his head. "You've much more understanding."

"Perhaps you weren't easy to understand, Dad."

Moore's face saddened. "Perhaps. But you try." He turned back into the big room. "Melva Cornish is still at the post, Harriet."

Her face tightened. "I thought she was going east."

He shook his head. "This time it's Ellis Morgan."

"And you're thinking that it will be Dan Fayes next?"

"Why not? It's always been the same. It was Jim Dunphy while he was CO. Morgan took command and Melva is commanding *him*. Now Ellis will go back to Company A. Give Melva a week and she'll be after Fayes."

She laughed bitterly. "Why wait a week?"

Moore watched her go to her room. He shook his head and mopped the bar.

Fort Costain sprawled across a mesa top like a raw-boned trooper sleeping off a tequila drunk. The sun reflected from the whitish caliche of the paradeground and glinted from the brass barrel of the stubby mountain howitzer which sat near the warped flagpole. The paradeground was lined on two sides by adobe barracks and quarters. The third side was composed of the stables and corrals with a row of sun-faded Sibley tents flapping and bellying in the hot wind. Shaggy ramadas shaded the fronts of the buildings while on the low roofs of the adobes vegetation had sprouted. Flash rains had cut deep gullies into the end of the paradeground where it dropped off in a steep escarpment to the creek bottoms to the east of the post proper. The post cemetery, on a low knoll, was perilously close to the deep gullies.

Dan eyed his command with some distaste. This was the post of duty which might save his shaky career. It was damned poor material from which to mold a model fort. Sherman had said Fort Costain had once been a key post in checking Apache ravages. There was little other reason for it to stand in stark nakedness on the sterile mesa top. In the distance, distorted by shimmering heat waves, rose the spectral mountains, the traditional stronghold of the rimrock Apaches.

Booth reined in the mules at the guardhouse. A trooper strolled out from beneath the shade of a ramada. His shirt showed white crescents of dried sweat beneath the armpits. He sported a day-old beard. The stock of his carbine had not felt the caress of a warm hand rubbing linseed oil into the walnut for many a day.

"Major Fayes, the new commanding officer, Krasner," said Booth.

Krasner eyed Dan and then gave him a sloppy salute. He pointed with his carbine toward a large adobe. "Headquarters. Captain Morgan has been expecting you, sir." He watched Dan through slitted eyes as the Dougherty rolled off.

Dan got down and slapped the dust from his clothing with his hat. 'Find my quarters, Booth and put my gear in them."

Booth saluted and drove off. Dan touched the orders in his inner coat pocket and walked into the dim orderly room. In an inner office a bulky officer sat at a desk, looking through a window toward the mountains. He turned as Dan entered. "Yes?"

"Major Fayes," said Dan. There was a half-empty bottle on Morgan's desk.

The man stood up and saluted. "Morgan," he said.

Dan sat down in a chair and felt for a cigar. Morgan had a full face with small eyes. His black mustache was trimmed dragoon style. It was obvious that the big man was suffering from the heat. Not enough time spent in the saddle, thought Dan.

"How was the trip?" asked Morgan.

"Hot and dry."

"It's always hot and dry," said Morgan sourly.

From his speech he was a Border State man, thought Dan. His eyes were red-rimmed. There was a weariness in his almost handsome face. Weariness from boredom rather than hard work. The appearance of the post proved that. Dan offered Morgan a cigar. They lit up.

"Would you like to meet the officers now, sir?" asked Morgan.

"Not just yet. Keep them at their duties. I'd like a talk with you before I take over."

Morgan nodded. He leaned back in his chair, sizing Dan up, as though he expected a rawhiding. Like a schoolboy caught in some mischief.

"You know why I was assigned here, Morgan?"

"Reform. Tighten up the squadron and all that."

"You don't think it can be done?"

"I did my best." There was an edge in his tone.

"Obviously it wasn't enough."

Morgan eyed the end of his cigar with great interest. "Shall I tell you what Cump Sherman told me about this post and the command?"

"What *did* they tell you, Major Fayes?"

"That it was rotten with insubordination. That the officers spent a great deal of time drinking and writing letters to their congressmen asking for transfers while they let the command go to hell." Dan puffed at his cigar. "But the worst part of the report was that the troopers acted like a bunch of rotten conscripts."

Morgan straightened up. "Did they tell you *all* of it, Major?" His face flushed. "Did they tell you that we've never been part of a regiment? That we've been in existence since '67, as a so-called provisional organization? Did they tell you we were sent out here to fight Apaches with the roster loaded with green recruits and only a small leavening of veterans to ease the strain? They probably didn't tell you about the fight at Negra Pass last year when most of the officers, with one or two exceptions, were fresh from the Point? Captain Reichert didn't come back from the slaughter. He preferred to die there rather than return to face the Benzine Board. And he was one of the best officers that ever forked a McClellan!"

Dan eyed the blustering officer. "I read the official report. I don't know the personal facts. But I do know this! This squadron will be built into an efficient organization and incorporated into a newly planned regiment or the men will be scattered to more efficient commands! I hardly need tell you what will happen to the officers!"

"Does that include you?"

"It does!"

Morgan hesitated. "I wish I could speak freely."

"Shoot."

The small eyes narrowed. "I expected a rawhiding from you. General Crook came through here after the Negra Pass fight. There was an unholy rawhiding then. But did he attempt to build up the morale? Did he order us to a more decent post where we could feel like we were part of the military picture?"

"Obviously not."

"No. Damn him! George Crook worries more about what the newspapers say about him than he does about how *we* feel about him. He surrounds himself with a bunch of border riffraff he calls mulepackers! He treats Apaches like humans! By God, Fayes, in six months he hasn't once mentioned this command."

"Probably with good reason," said Dan dryly.

Morgan gripped big fists together. "Well, the command is yours. I'm through. Do I take over A Company?"

"Your old command?"

"Yes."

"Take command again."

Morgan had a choleric temper beneath

his outward look of steadiness. "Anything else, sir?"

"Corporal Tanner has been killed and scalped. We found him beyond the pass."

Morgan paled. "The Apaches have been quiet."

"I've been told there have been smoke signals for some days."

"We see them now and then."

"Have you investigated them?"

Morgan flushed. "No."

"No scouting? No patrols?"

"No."

Dan stood up. He threw his orders on the desk. "We also met Black Wind. He had quite a lot to say about his people. It seems as though something is arousing them."

"The old man is blind. He hasn't been seen around here for years."

"He's around now."

Morgan bit his lip.

Dan left the building and crossed the sun-beaten paradeground to his quarters. He knew Morgan was watching him from a window. Booth was leaning against the wall of Dan's quarters. "Anything else, sir?"

"Not for the present. Take care of your team."

"You'll need an orderly, sir. I'd like the job."

"We'll see."

Dan walked through the hallway and into the lefthand room. Dust motes swirled in a shaft of sunlight streaming through a window. The beehive fireplace was littered with ashes and pieces of partially burned wood. The yellowed whitewash on the walls was streaked where water had leaked through the roof. Dust gritted beneath Dan's feet as he walked about. He sat down on the cot. Dust rose in a fine cloud around him.

Dan lit a fresh cigar. He knew now he should have told old Cump Sheridan to go to hell. Fourteen years of service and here he was, starting all over again. The army was like that. Work like hell on an assignment; get yanked from it when it's going well; start another dirty job.

Dan felt in his bag for the mezcal bottle.

Someone had swilled out of it. Booth. Dan shook his head. He uncorked the bottle and took a long drink. He needed it.

5

DAN spent the afternoon unpacking his luggage, setting Booth to work cleaning his weapons and brass. Across the narrow hallway was another room which Booth had told him had belonged to Major Dunphy. It had not been used since Dunphy had shot himself in it. Booth looked in at the dusty quarters. There was a dark stain on the packed-earth floor near the bare cot. Hanging on the wall was a tattered guidon which Booth told Dan had been the flag of Dunphy's company in the Shenandoah during the war.

Retreat was long past when Dan gathered his toilet articles and walked through the hallway to the rear door on his way to the washhouse. The first stars blinked in the dark blue blanket of the sky. The odor of cooking drifted across the post.

Dan bathed and shaved, taking his time, enjoying the sensation of the first real bath he had had since leaving St. Louis. Mess Call blew across the post. He threw his towel over his shoulder and blew out the candle lantern. The dry desert wind ruffled his hair as he stepped out into the darkness. The shadows in one place looked thicker. He slowed his pace. The shadow was a lot blacker and more solid than it should be. He reached out to touch it.

The shadow rose like an uncoiling spring. Dan caught the dull sheen of metal as he threw himself sideways. Something struck at the huck towel and stung his shoulder. The strong odor of sweat-soaked greasy leather clogged his nostrils. He brought up a knee, sinking it deep into his assailant's groin. The man grunted and went down.

Dan kicked out. His heel connected solidly. The man leaped to his feet and darted about the corner of the washhouse on silent feet.

Dan shook his head. It had been almost like a hallucination. Then his right foot struck something on the ground. He picked it up and held it close to his eyes. It was a thin-bladed knife, the haft bound tightly with rawhide. Dan walked into his quarters and turned up the lantern. His shoulder twinged. He threw aside the towel and pulled his undershirt free from his left shoulder. A shallow gash showed in the flesh in the hollow below the collarbone.

Dan wiped the cold sweat from his face. He poured mezcal on the cut and bandaged it. "The sonofabitch," he said. "Right on the post!"

He dressed carefully, slipping his derringer into his trousers pocket. He slanted his forage cap on his close-cropped head and blew out the lantern. He walked outside and breathed deep of the fresh air. It had been too damned close for peace of mind.

Lights from windows and doors threw their squares and rectangles on the hard earth. The flag halyards rattled violently against their warped pole. Dan crossed the paradeground to the officers' mess. It was well lit. A man laughed loudly as he pushed open the door.

Twelve officers came to their feet as someone called Attention. Dan walked to the head of the table. "Major Dan Fayes," he said quietly. "Please give your name, in order of rank, and present assignment."

Morgan did not speak. A broad-shouldered officer, with graying hair spoke up. "Captain Charles Norman, commanding Company B."

A smooth-faced man beside Charles was nex. "Captain Andrew Horace, commanding Company C."

"Captain Myron Cornish, surgeon."

The junior officers, four first and four second lieutenants, called off their names, rank and assignments.

Morgan turned to Dan. "First Lieutenant Dennis Halloran is in the hospital at Fort Grant with a case of varioloid fever, sir. He commanded Company A while I was acting post commander."

"Sit down, gentlemen," said Dan. He handed his cap to the mess orderly.

Morgan stood up. "Gentlemen, I'd like to propose a toast to our new post commander."

The orderly filled the wine glasses and the officers drank the toast. Dan picked up his glass and returned the honor. The wine was rather good. It seemed to hit him right where it did the most benefit.

The meal progressed swiftly. Second Lieutenant Forrest Kroft toyed with his food and kept draining his wineglass. By the time the meal was finished his face was flushed and a silly grin passed over it now and then.

Dan accepted a cigar from the box and lit up. The officers finished and eyed him expectantly. Dan spoke up. "Gentlemen, it is a pleasure to be here with you at Fort Costain. I realize it is not good manners to talk shop at mess, but tonight will be an exception."

Kroft bowed his head slightly.

Dan leaned forward. "Is it customary to be ambushed by Apaches within the confines of the post?"

"What the hell!" blurted Horace.

Kroft raised his glass. "Welcome to our select circle, Major Fayes. You've joined the ranks of the initiated."

"Shut up, Kroft," said Norman angrily.

Dan drew the knife from inside his

blouse and threw it on the table. "As I left the washhouse an Apache nearly tried to see to it that I left this world. Where are the guards? Do they let *broncos* have the run of the post after dark?"

Morgan flushed. "They're devils for that type of work, Major. Although it has been some time since anything like that has happened."

"We usually carry sidearms after dark," said Adjutant Nat Woodridge.

"Thanks for letting me know about that matter of routine," said Dan dryly. "Who is the officer of the guard?"

All eyes turned to Sid Sykes of Company A. Sykes stood up. He wore Colt and sword.

Dan jerked a thumb toward the door. "Get out there! Make the rounds! Double the guards if necessary. Tell Gila Barnes I want to see him."

Sykes saluted and hurried from the mess hall.

Dan placed his hands flat on the table. "I have a neat incision in my left shoulder, a souvenir of my first night on this J company post! I have been sent here to make a squadron out of this unit and I intend to do so. The alternative is the Benzine Board for every one of you seated here tonight!"

Horace wiped a fat hand over his full mouth. "May I say a word, sir?"

"Speak up."

Horace glanced along the table as though for support. "This is a hell of a place, sir. Out on the devil's hind leg. We've been given dregs for recruits. Jailbirds. Snowbirds. Runaway husbands. We haven't even got a regimental number to call our own. Why, sir, believe it or not, but twenty per cent of my company is either over the hill or in the brig!"

"No reflection on you, I hope," said Dan sarcastically.

Horace compressed his soft mouth. "Sir!"

Dan looked along the table. Kroft was leaning back in his chair swilling the wine around in his glass. There was a vacant look on his handsome face. "One of your own junior officers, Captain Horace, hasn't got the sense to drink like a gentleman at mess.

Yet you sit there and speak about your percentage of deserters and brig-birds as though it was their fault."

Horace stood up. "I do not like to be called down in front of junior officers!"

"Sit down!"

Morgan coughed. "Sir, it's true we have been a bit sloppy. Have we the promise of better men? Can we get new equipment?"

Dan shook his head. "You'll make or break the men you have. Congress hasn't seen fit to up the military appropriations bill. We'll get by on what we have." He stood up. "Corporal Tanner was ambushed and scalped five miles beyond the pass. We found his body this morning. There have been smoke signals for several days. Trouble is brewing in these hills and it's our job to stop it. I want a full field inspection tomorrow morning after stables."

Horace blinked. "The men won't be ready for it."

Dan eyed the flustered company commander. "See to it. Now, gentlemen, I have work to do, and I know you have. Good night."

The officers filed out. Dan drained his glass. Surgeon Cornish got his cap. He stopped beside Dan. "I'd better take a look at that shoulder," he said with a smile.

Dan nodded. Cornish wore the perpetual smile of a man who is always satisfied with himself. His dark eyes studied Dan through a cloud of tobacco smoke. He glanced down at the empty wineglass and then left the room.

Outside Dan stood for a moment letting the dry wind sweep about him. A stooped figure rounded the corner of the mess building. Gila Barnes stopped and shoved back his battered hat. The strong odor of tobacco and sweaty clothing vied with the fresh desert wind. "Yuh want to see me, Dan?"

They crossed the paradeground together. Dan told him of the Apache. Gila nodded. "I'll leave right away. God knows I won't catch up with him, but I been wantin' to poke about the hills."

"How often has something like this happened?"

Gila spat. "Not for some time. Halloran was jumped once. Drilled the bushy-headed bastard with a slug. Denny is a cool man."

Dan nodded. "Take off then."

Gila saluted and vanished toward the stables. Dan went into his quarters and lit the lamp. He had been rough on his officers, but four years of war, and the years of duty as an inspector, hadn't taught him any other system. The wine worked in him. He picked up the bottle of mezcal and drank deeply. He stripped off his shirt and undershirt and sat down on his bunk. He drew his revolving pistol from its holster and twirled the cylinder. The click of steel sounded loud in the stillness. He placed the Colt on the small table near the head of his bed.

The outer door opened. "Major Fayes!" called Cornish.

"Come in, Doc!"

Cornish was carrying his medical bag. A woman followed him in. Dan reached for his shirt. Cornish smiled. "It's all right, Major. This is my sister, Melva. She's used to things like this. Helps me a lot. A good steady hand with the wounded or the sick." Cornish busied himself with his case.

Melva Cornish was a tall woman in her middle twenties. Her dark eyes held Dan's as she extended a hand. "Welcome to Fort Costain, Major."

"Thank you, Miss Cornish."

The faint odor of heliotrope had entered the room. Melva Cornish was full-bosomed, her breasts thrusting themselves out tightly against her dark dress. Her black hair was swept up and carefully arranged. Her mouth was full and ripe. She exerted a slight pressure on Dan's hand before she released it. Her eyes took in his muscular upper body and then the hastily bandaged shoulder. Dan suddenly had a feeling he had known someone like her before, in a place where a lady would have felt ill at ease.

"Take off the bandage, Melva," said Myron Cornish over his shoulder.

She came close to Dan and unfastened the bandage. Her cool fingers felt good on his warm flesh. "I heard you picked up Corporal Tanner on the way here."

"Yes." Dan looked away. He didn't want to talk about it.

Cornish looked up. "Neat job. Tanner's mutilation. Takes an expert to do it right. They never tear or peel it off. A quick incision to the bone and then a straight upward pull." He thrust his left thumb into his mouth and popped his cheek. "Like that!"

Dan eyed the surgeon distastefully. Melva patted Dan's shoulder. "There," she said easily. She looked at her brother. "I agree with you, Myron. It was a nice job."

"You saw it?" asked Dan.

She raised her thick eyebrows. "Of course! They brought the body into the dispensary."

Dan felt the need for a drink.

Cornish worked deftly. The strong odor of carbolic filled the room. Melva bandaged swiftly. As she moved Dan could feel the swell of her full thigh against his left leg. He looked at her. She flushed a little and stepped back. "Thanks," said Dan.

She smiled. "I like to help," she said. "Heaven knows there isn't much else to do here at Fort Costain."

"A rough place for a woman," said Dan.

Cornish grinned. "Melva likes it," he said.

Dan drew his shirt about his shoulders. "Drink?"

Cornish nodded. Dan filled two glasses. They downed the potent mezcal. Dan found his eyes wandering toward the full-bodied Melva. By God, she *was* a woman, double-breasted and firm.

Cornish eyed his empty glass. "Good stuff," he said. "I noticed the odor of it when I came in here."

"I cleansed the wound with it."

Cornish nodded. "Good stuff, inside or out. In moderation, of course." The dark eyes studied Dan for a moment. "Well, I have work to do. Coming Melva?"

She nodded. As she walked to the door her hips swung easily. Dan put down his glass. A few more drinks and he would have followed her.

Dan dropped on his bunk. They were a queer pair. Then he remembered who Melva reminded him of. Kitty St. Clair in

Washington. Kitty had fitted well in Dolly Aldon's establishment in the capital city. Kitty had spurned a wealthy congressman to give all her attentions to Dan. He closed his eyes. He wished that Kitty was with him now.

6

BY noon of the day after Dan's arrival at Fort Costain he knew the squadron was almost as rotten as the post buildings. The inspection had been a farce. Carbine barrels were pitted, although none of the weapons were more than three years old, issue of 1869. In all three company barracks he had seen but half a dozen pairs of boots that looked like they had been shined. Cots were sloppily made. Uniforms had been superficially spruced. Dan learned that the company commanders made a practice of keeping the company Colts locked in boxes in their quarters, for on the frontier, Colts were better than currency, and most of the men could not be trusted with them.

Dan walked into headquarters. Adjutant Woodridge was still busy with the inspection records in C Company barracks. At Dan's request, Amos Linke, the squadron clerk, silently placed a bundle of service records before him. Dan scanned through them. The list of deserters was scandalously high. Drunkenness and insubordination topped the list of crimes for which men were confined in the guardhouse. Dan sat down and lit a cigar. He looked at Linke, a slight unsoldierly-looking man with thin graying hair. "Where's the sergeant major?"

Linke looked up. "Over the hill. Sergeant Major Haley."

"Hell," said Dan involuntarily, "him too?"

Linke nodded.

Dan flipped over the papers until he found Haley's record. He whistled softly. Twenty-seven years with the colors. Battles and campaigns: Mexican War, Civil War, and half a dozen Indian campaigns. Wounded four times. Cited three times for gallantry in action.

Linke coughed. "Sergeant Haley is a hard violent man but a splendid soldier. There is none better. For a time he tried to keep up the efficiency of the squadron, but it could not be done by *one* man. Haley turned to steady drinking. One night at Moore's Hog Ranch, he went raving mad from the liquor. When the fight was over three civilians were badly beaten and Mike Haley went over the hill."

"Quite the bucko boy."

Linke smiled proudly as though Haley's sins were a thing he took pride in. "That he is. But a finer soldier, with drill, paper-work, fighting or any other part of the soldier's trade, there never was."

Dan puffed at his cigar. "You speak as though you've had an education, Linke. How do you account for Haley?"

Linke smiled. "Each of us is cast in a mold at birth, sir. Lawyer, doctor, beggar-man or thief. Haley was *born* a soldier. But in him there is a flaw . . . for a soldier, that is. There is a sensitivity in him. Put him in a good unit and he'll make it better. Put him in a bad one and he'll make it good. But in him there is the same feeling we all of us have. Pride in our unit, and to hell with all the others, begging your pardon, sir." Linke shook his head. "His patience ran out here. Why else would he, a born soldier, do the one thing you'd expect from a nonmilitary man?"

Dan winced inwardly at the quiet words of the scholarly clerk. "It seems unanswerable. Where is he?"

Linke looked away.

"Come on! He must have been your good friend for you to know him so well and praise him so highly. *Where is he?*"

Linke looked squarely at Dan. "And if I tell the major, what will he do? Break his spirit in the guardhouse with the scum that inhabits it now? Shave half his head and drum him off the post to the tune of the Rogue's March?"

Dan shook his head. "I give you my word."

Linke smiled. "He is at Union, on the upper San Ignacio, twenty miles from here."

Dan did some quick calculating. "I'll leave here on a three-day pass. Reason: post business. Write that down." Dan stood up. "Captain Morgan will assume command in my absence." He looked at Linke. "I'm curious about you. You do not talk like the average yellowleg."

Linke flushed. "I had a fine education, sir. But it taught me nothing of liquor and gambling." The little man smiled ruefully. "If there were no drunkards amongst educated men, sir, the army would have no fourteen-dollar-a-month clerks."

Dan left headquarters, and met Morgan crossing the paradeground.

"I'm leaving the post for a few days. Take over in my absence."

Morgan was startled. "For what reasons, may I ask?"

"Official business. Jack up this squadron, Captain Morgan. I want no repetition of this morning's inspection."

Morgan bit his lip. "A peace commissioner from the Indian Bureau is due soon."

"Let him wait."

Morgan eyed Dan.

Dan flipped away his cigar. "I want you to start officer and NCO schools three nights a week. I want every man to fire for record starting tomorrow. Ninety rounds. Wingate's *Manual of Rifle Practice*. There will be full-dress parade at retreat until further orders."

Dan walked away leaving Morgan staring after him. He entered his quarters. Booth was whitewashing the walls. The ripe full odor of mezcal floated in the air even above the odor of the whitewash. Dan picked up his mezcal bottle. It was empty. "Booth," he said.

Booth turned. "Oh *that*, sir. I kicked it over by mistake."

Dan threw the bottle into the fireplace. "You misbegotten drunken bastard! Get me a horse. A good one. Fill a canteen. Bring him here."

"I'll get you Hardtack. One of A Company's bays."

Dan changed into an old pair of issue trousers and shirt. He pulled on his field boots and picked up his Winchester. Booth stuck his head in through the window. "All set, sir."

Dan walked outside and placed his blanket roll over the cantle. Booth tied it fast. Dan swung up on Hardtack and touched the big bay with his spurs. It was damned good to be in a McClellan again. A good ride would blow the stink of Fort Costain from his nostrils. He acknowledged the salute of the gate sentry and rode slowly down the winding road to the Mesquite Wells road.

Moore's Ranch seemed to be dreaming in the hot afternoon sun. Dan kneed Hardtack onto the short road that led up to the buildings. He slid from the saddle and walked in. The big room was empty. He walked to the bar and called out.

Harriet Moore, dressed in a simple gingham dress, came from a back room. "Hello, Major," she said.

"The name is Dan."

"Dan then."

He eyed her. She had changed her hair style, drawing it back from her oval face, and piling it on top of her shapely head. Her slim, full-bosomed figure fitted into the simple dress as though she had been poured into it. She flushed a little. "You're not leaving so soon?"

He shook his head. "How do I get to Union?"

She looked at him queerly. "Follow the road through Mesquite Wells. Beyond the town there is a fork, one leading northwest toward Beasley. The right-hand fork follows the San Ignacio. Union is about twenty miles up the valley."

"Thanks, Miss Moore."

She smiled. "The name is Harriet."

They eyed each other, and Dan suddenly knew what he had been missing while at the fort. "Is everything all right?" he asked.

"Yes. With me. Dad's feelings aren't so good right now."

"How so?"

"One of his teamsters was fired at in the hills. He got away from the wagon and hid. When he came back he found that the wagon was looted."

"Who did it?"

"We don't really know. Apaches probably."

"What was in the wagon?"

"Flour. Bacon. Dried fish. Some reloading tools. Blasting powder. Three cases of

Henry rifle ammunition."

Dan rubbed his jaw. "I'd like a report from your father when he gets back."

"I'll tell him."

Dan turned toward the door. "I'll only be gone a few days, Harriet."

"Be careful." She followed him to the door and winced a little when she saw the horse. "Hardtack," she said.

Dan eyed her. "So?"

"That was Jim Dunphy's favorite mount."

"I see." Dan mentally cursed Trooper Booth. "I didn't know."

She leaned against the side of the door. "It doesn't matter."

Dan swung up on the bay. He raised his campaign hat.

"I hope Mike Haley is still there," she said.

Dan lowered his hat and rested an elbow on his pommel. "Why did you say that?"

She tilted her head to one side. "Mike Haley is the best soldier Fort Costain ever saw. You need him. But be careful with him, Dan."

"Why?"

She straightened up. "He's a strong man with strong opinions."

"I have some strong opinions myself."

"Yes," she said quietly.

Dan touched the bay with his spurs and rode down toward the road. He looked back. The wind whipped her skirts about her long slim legs. There was a strange disquieting feeling within him. He looked back twice more before he reached a curve in the road. She was still standing there looking after him.

Union sprawled like an ugly excrescence on a pitted slope beneath shabby mine structures. Warped false-fronted buildings lined a dusty main street. Ore wagons groaned down the hill from the mines heading for the stamp mills Dan had seen three miles down the creek road.

Leaving the bay in the town's one livery stable, he walked up the street and entered the first saloon he saw, the Big Garrel. He ordered a beer and eyed the few other customers. Most of them looked like miners. None of them had the Regular Army stamp on them.

The batwings swung open and a thick-bodied man came in with his head lowered as though he were primed for violent action. His slab of a face had the imprint of Erin on it. His blue eyes were red-rimmed and his mahogany face was covered with russet bristles. A filthy flannel shirt, open to the belly, showed a thick mat of reddish hair on the deep chest. His sleeves were rolled up on his powerful arms, exposing a Maltese cross tattoed on the left forearm. The insignia of the old Fifth Corps. There had been ten regiments of Regulars in the Fifth, commanded by George Sykes. Sykes's Regulars.

The bartender eyed him warily. "You've got no more jawbone here, Haley."

Haley lowered his bullethead. "So me credit is no good, you scut? I've thrown one hundred eagles across this mahogany in the past few days and ye'll give me no jawbone?"

The bartender shook his head.

"Throw the bum out!" a big miner

roared from a poker table.

Haley turned slowly. His powerful hands gripped the bar behind him. "Now who said that?" he asked quietly.

The miner dropped his hands below the table. Dan could see a derringer in one of them. Dan slid his Colt free from the leather. "You there," he said clearly, "put away that stingy gun!"

All eyes turned toward Dan. Haley stared at him. The bartender leaned across the bar. "If he's a friend of yours, stranger, get him outa here. There's been a fight every night he's been in here and that hairy Irishman didn't lose one of them. There'll be a killin' if he ain't stopped."

Dan nodded. "Come on, Irish," he said, "let's go get a drink elsewhere."

There was suspicion on the homely face but Haley, surprisingly enough, preceded him out into the darkening street. "Thanks," he said over his shoulder, "I did not see the gun."

"It would have been the last reveille for you, Haley."

Haley rubbed his bristly jaw. "Where to?"

"I've got a bottle at the livery stable."

Haley threw a heavy arm about Dan's shoulders. His breath was like a rusty blade. "There's something familiar about ye. Something I do not rightly place."

The street was dark, lit only by the yellow light shining through dirty windows. Dan jerked his head. "The livery is down there."

Haley seemed satisfied. "There is a girl in Molly's who can give a man a fine go-around. Ye're interested?"

"Later perhaps."

They stopped in front of the livery stable. The big bay was in a rear stall. The liveryman was nowhere in sight. Haley swayed a little as he walked toward the back. He eyed the bay. "This horse is familiar," he said thickly.

Dan eased his Colt free and raised it.

Haley stared at the horse. "By God! 'Tis Hardtack!"

The heavy gun barrel struck just above Haley's left ear. The big man crumpled at the knees and went down like a falling pine.

"Timber!" said Dan. He dragged the non-com into the darkness and went to look for the liveryman.

He met the man walking toward the stable picking at his teeth with a straw.

Dan took out his wallet. "I want a horse," he said. "I'm taking a friend back to Fort Costain."

"I've got a gelding with one eye. Give him to you for thirty dollars."

"It's a deal."

They walked back to the stable. Dan saddled the rawboned gelding. The liveryman helped him place Haley over the saddle.

Two miles from Union Dan stopped and dismounted. He stripped off his clothing and replaced it with worn cavalry trousers and a shell jacket. He remounted Hardtack.

The moon was up when Haley moved and groaned. Dan led the gelding down to the shallow creek and untied Haley. He lowered the big man to the ground and splashed water on his face. Haley opened one eye. "Hellfire!" he said. "That last drink was a howitzer shell!" He looked up at Dan. "For the love av Saint Patrick! Who the hell are you?"

"Major Dan Fayes, the new commanding officer of Fort Costain."

Haley jumped to his feet. "I have no CO, Mister. What's goin' on?"

Dan grinned. "You've been kidnaped, Haley. You're coming back to the blue where you belong."

Haley shook his head and worked his mouth, trying to free it from the fur. "Ah, to hell with that! They are not soldiers there. It is a reform school and the officers are but lazy men who do not care about the squadron. I'm well out of it."

"You're coming back."

"To be thrown in a cell? No!"

"You owe me a favor. If you come back I'll see to it that you don't go in a cell."

Haley squinted at Dan. "Ye're a strange one. Ye do have the look of a man and a soldier. But it is too late."

"Then I'll take you back at gunpoint."

"You?" Haley laughed. "I could crush ye wid one fist."

Dan grinned. "I'll strip off this coat and we'll settle it right here. If I win, you come back. If you win, you take the gelding, fifty eagles, and my blessing."

Haley grinned craftily. "Ye're a man right enough. Come. I'll go easy on ye. I'll not mark ye up. I'll put ye to sleep easy-like."

Dan stripped off his gunbelt, cap and shell jacket. The moon was bright and clear. He had never been licked in his weight class at the Point, but Haley had thirty pounds on him. Dan had youth on his side. Haley had John Barleycorn riding his back, slowing him down.

Haley shuffled his big feet and spat on his hands. He moved in ponderously, his pale blue eyes alight with battle. Dan moved about, studying the man. He was powerful, but there was a layer of fat about his middle. He was at least forty-five years old. Suddenly the Irishman closed in, throwing short hard punches, making no attempt to hit Dan.

Dan moved back. Haley grinned and moved in. Dan speared out a left and jolted home a smashing right to the gut. Haley's whisky breath came out in a gush. Haley bobbed about, trying to clear his head. The liquor was still strong in him, although he wasn't really drunk. Haley feinted. A granite fist grazed Dan's jaw and another whizzed past his chin.

Dan moved about.

"Stand still, damn ye . . . *sir!*"

Dan threw a left. He threw a right which Haley easily blocked. He countered with a left to Dan's lean belly and skidded a right across Dan's jaw. The blow was enough to start dancing lights in front of Dan. The man was as rough as a cob. The blow which grounded him seemed to come from nowhere. Dan went down hard and looked up at the grinning NCO.

"Time," said Haley.

Dan got to his feet. He tapped Haley three more times and then went staggering back with a vicious right over the heart. He went down on one knee.

"Had enough?" asked Haley.

Dan shook his head. He sparred easily, keeping away from the sledgehammer blows. Haley was puffing. Haley lost his temper, triggered by a stinging left to the eye. He charged. Dan's forearms ached from the pistonlike blows.

Dan sank home a left to the gut and followed through with a jolting uppercut which snapped the bullethead back. He followed through with a left to the jaw and a short right. Dan knew he had broken a knuckle as he looked down at Haley. "Time," he said.

Haley shook his head. There was a pale sickness on his face. He got to his feet and swung a hard right. Dan went under it, clipped Haley on the jaw with a left and sent him down again with a right jab.

Haley wiped the blood from his mouth. Doggedly he got up. Dan was after him like a wolverine. Haley covered up and retreated. His heel caught on a root just as Dan timed a smashing right to the jaw.

Haley went flat. His eyes closed and opened. "It's the liquor," he said.

"No alibis, Haley."

Haley sat up and felt his jaw. "I could lick ye if I was in shape."

"You're right there."

Haley grinned. "Few men have ever downed me, drunk *or* sober. Ye're a good man wid yer dukes, Mister Fayes."

Dan leaned against his bay. "You're coming back then?"

Haley stood up. "Yes. We made a bargain. 'Twill be hell not wearin' me stripes."

"We'll see about that."

Haley squatted by the creek and slopped water on his face. "Ye're a quare one, sir. I'm thinking we'll have some soldiering at Costain from now on."

"We'll try."

The big mick stood up. "Aye, that we will."

Dan swung up on Hardtack. "Boots and saddles, Haley."

They rode back to the road and headed south.

7

IT was almost noon when Dan drew rein in front of Moore's Ranch. Haley slid from his saddle and eyed the main building. He wiped his mouth on a hairy forearm. Dan shook his head. "There will be no drinking."

"Ah, sir!"

Dan slapped the dust from his uniform. "We made a deal," he said.

"When does it end, Major?"

Dan grinned. "When you get your stripes back."

"That may be a long time, sir."

"It may be."

The light blue eyes studied Dan. "You're not a drinking man yourself, sir?"

"At times."

Dan walked into the big saloon room. Jim Moore looked up from the bar. "I'm glad to see you back, Fayes," he said.

"How so?"

Moore came around the end of the bar. "I'm worried. Bertram Morris, a peace commissioner, arrived yesterday at Fort Costain. He went on to the reservation to meet with the Apaches. Captain Morgan sent Captain Horace and his company along."

"So?"

Moore shook his head. "I've known Morris for some time. He believes implicitly that the Apaches are well enough off at San Ignacio Reservation. He'll give them nothing. Morris is a small man, in stature and in mind. The Apaches hate him. He was the wrong man to send. Besides, Horace has an ungodly fear of the Apaches. If trouble starts he'll handle it wrongly. I'm sure of that."

Haley nodded his head. "He's right there, sir."

Dan lit a cigar. "When did they leave?"

"Shortly after noon. They'll be there by now."

Dan walked toward the door. "Come on, Haley. Do you know the way to the reservation?"

"Yes, sir!"

They mounted and rode on to the fort. The steady thump of carbine fire came from the range along the shallow creek. Haley cocked his head. "That's a sound I haven't heard for some time," he said. "Ye've done well for yer short time here, sir."

Dan dismounted at headquarters. "Stay here," he said. He walked in. Adjutant Woodridge was at his desk. "Glad to see you back, sir. Is that Mike Haley out there?"

"It is."

Woodridge shook his head. "I never thought anyone could bring *him* back."

"Tell Captain Morgan to come to my quarters."

Woodridge nodded.

"I'm leaving for the reservations right after I see Morgan." He left the building. "Haley," he said, "Get into uniform. Get two fresh horses, and bring them to my quarters."

"Yes, sir!"

Dan was shaving when Morgan appeared. The big officer's eyes were clouded with sleep. Having a siesta, thought Dan. "I brought Sergeant Haley back," he said over his shoulder.

"So? I'll have him put in the guard-house."

Dan shook his head. "I'm taking him with me to the reservation."

"Why? Horace can handle it."

"Maybe. I want to hear what Morris has to say."

Morgan leaned against the wall. "He'll say plenty because you weren't here to meet him." Morgan's dark eyes studied Dan. "Bertram Morris has a lot of influence in Arizona, Major."

"Let's hope he has some with the Apaches."

Morgan laughed shortly. "They'll get nothing from him but big words and promises."

"Why did you send Horace in charge of the escort?"

"B Company is on guard. A is firing on the range."

Dan wiped his face and pulled on a fresh shirt.

Morgan lit a cigar. "You sound as though you don't like my choice of C Company for the escort."

"I didn't say that."

Morgan eyed Dan through a cloud of tobacco smoke. "Your tone did."

"All right then!" said Dan hotly, "I *didn't* like your choice. This may be a ticklish business. Horace didn't impress me as an officer who would keep his head under difficulties."

"It didn't take you long to form opinions of your officers."

Dan buckled on his gunbelt and picked up his Winchester. "I've no time to talk about it," he said.

Morgan threw his cigar into the fireplace. "You don't seem to like anything on this post. Officers or men."

Dan walked to the door. "What's on your mind, Morgan? Get on with it."

The secretive eyes shifted. "You're in a hurry. This can wait."

Dan walked outside. Haley was leading up two fresh horses. A woman walked beside him. It was Melva Cornish, the strong wind pressing her dress to her full figure, outlining the deep breasts and the full thighs. She stopped beside Dan. "You're not leaving so soon, Dan?" she asked.

"Yes, Melva."

She bit her full lip. "I had planned a party for you tonight. Will you be back in time?"

He fastened his Winchester to the saddle. "I don't know."

"Well, perhaps we can plan it when you return."

He nodded. "That will be fine, Melva." His mind was far from parties and the ripe body of Melva Cornish. Then he saw the smoldering eyes of Ellis Morgan fixed on the young woman and he knew what was nettling the big officer.

The carbines thumped on the range and a cloud of smoke drifted up from the creek bottoms. Dan swung up on his bay and lifted his hat to Melva. Haley followed him as he rode toward the gate. Dan glanced at the noncom. Haley's left knuckles were skinned. They hadn't been that way the last time Dan had seen him. "You've cut your hand, Haley," he said.

Haley grinned. "The major doesn't miss much," he said. "I fell up against a tree."

"Yes," said Dan quietly. "There are a hell of a lot of trees on Fort Costain."

They passed the gate and Dan handed the ex-noncom a cigar. They both lit up. Haley drew the smoke deep into his lungs. "'Twas Trooper Skillings," he said. "Now Skillings always had the idea he could best me in a Donnybrook if I was not sergeant major. He didn't."

Dan nodded. "It's not easy to go back with the other men once you've been a sergeant major," he said.

"How the mighty have fallen, Skillings said. Trooper Skillings did a little falling himself." Haley touched the dark area on his faded shirt where his stripes had been. "All the same, sir, I feel a bit indacint riding about without me stripes."

"You'll get them back."

Haley shrugged. "I do not want them unless they are earned."

"What ever gave you the thought that you'd get them any other way?"

The sun was low down in the west when Dan drew rein on the ridge that overlooked the winding, shallow waters of San Ignacio Creek. Smoke drifted up and then hung in a low cloud over the shadowy bottoms. The cavalry horses were picketed to the north on a grassy area. A row of cook fires glowed along the creek where the troopers of C Company were cooking their issue bacon in the spiders. The rich odor of bacon and coffee came up the ridge of the two men. Haley shifted in his saddle and eased his crotch. "The reservation proper is beyont that far ridge. This is the place where the bucks have their dances and soirees."

Almost directly below them were a number of wickiups, formed of thick whips of ocotillo, covered with skins and government blankets. A fire glowed in front of the biggest of them. Half a dozen men sat about the fire. Three of them, were white men. Bertram Morris, Captain Horace and a third man he did not recognise. Dan touched the bay with his spurs and guided it down the brushy slope. "This place smells of trouble," said Haley quietly behind him.

"You're thinking too much, Haley." But Dan felt a cold sensation travel down his back. He eased his Colt in its holster.

"Ye feel it too, sir?"

"Yes," said Dan quietly.

The men about the fire turned toward Dan as he rode out of the shadows. He dismounted silently and let Haley take the horses to the picket lines. Horace flushed as he recognized the CO. He stood up. "This is Mister Morris, Major Fayes," he said nervously, indicating the little man who sat beside him.

Morris did not get up. He turned a petulant face toward Dan. "I expected to find you at Fort Costain," he said in an irritated voice.

Dan eyed the smooth, round face. The eyes were small. Dan suddenly had the impression he was looking at an angry porker. Morris' hands scrabbled at his plump thighs.

A lean civilian squatted beside Morris. "Ducey," he introduced himself, "interpreter." He was a man without an ounce of fat on his gaunt frame. Neatly dressed in sober black. A Sharps rifle leaned against a rock behind him.

Dan nodded. The three Apaches that faced the government commissioner were old men, wrinkled and skinny. Ducey looked at them. "These men are Cut Lip, Yellow Bear and Long Hat. Cut Lip is the chief." Ducey turned to the three impassive Tontos and spoke in swift slurring Apache. They eyed Dan and then looked at Morris.

Morris loosened his high collar. "The fools are angry," he said over his shoulder to Dan. "They present impossible demands."

"Be careful," said Ducey. "They understand English much better than they let on."

Dan squatted beside Ducey. Beyond the big wickiup were four warriors, squatting on the ground, idly watching the conference. There were no others in sight. Dan looked beyond them. The far ridge was thick with brush. There was no sign of life on it. A cool wind swept down the valley, chilling him.

Horace shifted a little and lit a cigar. "I

don't like the smell of this, Major," he said.

Dan shook his head as Cut Lip spoke. At some time in his life the Tonto had been hideously maimed by a slash across his upper lip. The flesh had drawn back in a thick scar revealing the even white teeth. Ducey listened and then turned to Morris. "Cut Lip says that his people do not want trouble, but that they were promised blankets for the winter cold. They never came. They were promised fat beef cattle and received instead skinny beasts hardly fit for the teeth of a coyote. Do they get more promises or do they get thick blankets and fat cattle?"

Morris wet his lips. "Tell him that the government has spent much money at San Ignacio. Building houses. Barns. Supplying clothing."

Ducey translated. Cut Lip's eyes flashed. He spoke again. "Cut Lip says his people do not live in the white men's lodges. That the coughing and spitting sickness comes upon the children. That the clothing was old and dirty, hardly fit for The People to wear. That the Tontos want permission to hunt in the mountains as they always have. Digging in the earth is not for the Tontos. They are hunters."

Morris cleared his throat. "There has been trouble in the hills. Men have been killed. Wagons have been robbed. Ask him if he knows who has done this thing?"

Ducey paled a little beneath his tan. "It isn't Cut Lip who is responsible, Mister Morris," he said.

"Ask him!" Morris' voice cracked a little.

Ducey looked at Dan. "I don't like to, sir."

"Then you'd better not."

Morris turned with all the outraged dignity of the little man who thinks a bigger man is overbearing him. "Sir! This is my duty. To track down these troubles."

"You'll get more than you bargained for."

The bluish lips drew back from the discolored teeth. "And what has the army done about these troubles in the hills?"

Dan relit his cigar. "We're working on it, Mister Morris."

"Pah!" Morris turned away in disgust. He looked at Ducey. "Ask him."

Ducey looked at Dan. Dan shrugged. Ducey translated in a low voice. Cut Lip fingered his hideous scar. Then he spoke slowly.

"Cut Lip says his people had nothing to do with the trouble in the hills. They want peace. Hair Rope is behind the troubles."

"Then Hair Rope must be turned over to the authorities!"

Cut Lip digested this. He spoke to Yellow Bear and Long Hat. There was feral hate in the liquid eyes of the old men as they spoke to each other. Cut Lip stood up. "There is nothing we can do," he said. "Hair Rope left us many grasses ago. Can we be responsible for what he has done?"

Morris smashed a pudgy fist into a damp palm. "Hair Rope must be brought to justice! Tell that old man that there will be no more cattle! No blankets! No food unless we get Hair Rope!"

Dan stood up. Tension settled over the little group. Suddenly Dan noticed that the four warriors who had been seated behind the wickiup had vanished into the lengthening shadows. He looked down toward the bivouac. Two troopers were wrestling in a cleared area, spurred on by the jibes of their mates. There wasn't a sentry in the area. There was no sign of the junior officers of the company, Cliff Rosin and Forrest Kroft. Dan stepped back from the fire. The shadows along the ridge seemed alive with impending danger and he had a naked feeling as though many eyes were on the group about the fire.

Cut Lip listened to Ducey. Then he stood up. "The little White-eye wants Hair Rope," he said coldly. "Then he shall have him." He turned to Yellow Bear and spoke tensely. "Get him."

Yellow Bear trotted off into the darkness. Horace grinned. "I knew damned well they wouldn't start any trouble," he said.

"My God!" said Ducey.

A silence fell over the valley, broken only by the distant cries of the wrestling troopers. Dan stepped back into the shadows. Morris dabbled at his round face with a bandanna. "A firm hand, Major," he said, "a firm hand."

"Yes," said Dan absently. There was a smell of trouble in the evening air.

The rifle cracked flatly from the western ridge, a spurt of orange-red in the shadows. Morris grunted. He turned, pawing at his back. "I," he said, "I . . ." Then he pitched forward across the dying fire as the echo of the shot slammed back and forth across the valley.

Dan jumped behind a rock. Ducey cursed as he sprinted for cover. The smell of burning cloth rose from Morris' clothing. Then all hell broke loose in the shadows. A ripple of rifle fire raced along both ridges. The wrestling troopers had stopped, looking toward the treaty fire. One of them sagged in the arms of the man who held him. Then his late opponent went down, dragging the wounded man with him.

Dan suddenly noticed that Cut Lip and Long Hat had vanished. He drew his Colt. "Get to your command, Horace!" he yelled. He darted to the fire and dragged Morris from the flames. Slugs whipped over his head. The cavalry horses whinnied and screamed in sudden panic. Some of them broke free, whipping their picket pins from the soft earth. A group of them thundered down the valley. The troopers scattered for cover as leaden sleet poured into them. Half a dozen of them were down, lying still or thrashing in agony.

Dan knelt beside Morris. The little man's eyes were open but they did not see. Dan jumped into the brush. Something moved near him and he cocked his Colt. It was Andy Horace. Then the officer was gone.

Sporadic carbine fire broke out from the troopers. Dan heard Haley's bull voice lashing at them. He plunged through the scrub trees and brush. A lean figure rose from the darkness and whirled, raising a rifle. Dan fired twice from the hip, leaped the fallen figure and snatched up his rifle. It was a new Henry rifle. Dan holstered his Colt and darted into thick brush, levering home a round. He fired at a shadowy figure and was rewarded with a muffled shriek.

Rifle fire poured down from the ridges.

Dan dropped to his knees and crawled behind a rock ledge. A trooper turned and saw him. "God, sir," he said with gaping mouth, "we're sitting ducks."

"Shut up and shoot," said Dan.

Haley was driving the panicky troopers into cover. Then the rifle died away. Dan looked over the ledge. With the exception of the two Apaches he had fired at, there was not another buck in sight. He crawled to Haley. The big trooper spat. "Dammit," he said, "there ain't an officer with the men."

"Where are Kroft and Rosin?"

Haley gripped his carbine. "Corporal Denton said they rode over to the reservation to see the squaws."

Dan stared at the bitter man. "The fat's in the fire for sure. Morris is dead."

"Aye, and seven troopers are down." Haley threw a shot up the ridge. He flipped open the breech. The hot hull tinkled against a rock. "What now, sir?"

"Dig in. Below those rocks. Tell those damned noncoms to get control of their men."

Haley nodded and crawled off.

The valley was silent now. The fires glowed against the darkness. A horse whinnied up the valley. Dan crawled to the scattered company. Haley was lashing the noncoms into action. Gradually the company drew together. They piled rocks into a rude breastwork. Dan looked down the valley. Morris' feet protruded from behind a rock. There was no sign of life.

Haley squatted beside Dan. "What now, Mister Fayes?"

"They'll not fight at night."

"Aye, sir, but there's still the dawn to come. Shall I go back to the post for more men?"

"I'll go," a quiet voice said. Ducey appeared from the shadows.

"Look!" said Haley.

A squat Apache appeared on a rock, outlined against the western sky. "White-eyes!" he called. "You wanted Hair Rope! I am here!" Then he was gone as a cupful of slugs smashed about the rocks.

Dan felt a sickness within him. "Can you make it to the post, Ducey?"

"I think so."

"Go then. Bring a company if the post is safe. But for God's sake, tell them to watch for an ambush."

Ducey nodded and snaked off into the darkness.

Haley watched the interpreter until he was out of sight. "I've set a guard on the remaining horses, sir."

Metal clinked against gravel as the shattered company dug in. The troopers worked with the few spades they had as well as mess knives, plates and their bare hands. In an hour they were partially below-ground. A pale moon began to rise in the east. There was no movement on the overlooking ridges.

Dan placed his back against a rock and looked at the Henry rifle he had picked up. It was new. There had been other repeaters churning out death from the ridges.

"What about Lieutenants Kroft and Rosin, sir?" asked Haley.

Dan shrugged. He had no hope for them. But he had seen Captain Horace skulking in the shadows. There had been plenty of time for him to get back to his company. "Tell the men to get some sleep. Double guards. No shooting unless they're sure of a target, Haley."

"Yes, sir!"

Dan wanted a smoke but he satisfied himself by breaking up a cigar and chewing it. He had a full-sized outbreak on his hands now.

8

"WAKE-up, sir. 'Tis the false dawn."

Dan opened his eyes and shivered in the cold wind. Faint gray light was creeping into the valley of the San Ignacio. All about him he could see the sprawled troopers. Four of them lay near the stream that chuckled over its smooth stones. Haley had crawled out during the night with Corporal Denton to bring in the wounded.

"Trooper Wanska died durin' the night," said Haley. "Trooper Seligman has a slug in his chest. He's in a bad way. Troopers Lowell and Felton are hit hard but they will live."

Dan rubbed the sleep from his eyes and accepted a canteen from Haley. He drank sparingly. Haley brought out a twist of tobacco. "Chew, sir? It holds off the hunger for a smoke."

Dan nodded.

Haley handed him the cable twist. "'Tis Wedding Cake. Strong, but the sauce ain't too bad."

Dan cut off a chew and stowed it in his mouth. "Anything stirring?"

"'Tis quiet as the grave, sir."

Dan looked across the creek and then sat up straight. A man was there, propped against a tree. He had been stripped. The head was drawn back tight against the tree trunk with a length of rope. The eyes stared across the creek. There was a curious lop-sided look about the battered head. It had been crushed by a terrific blow. The naked body had been ripped open, letting the greasy entrails hang out over the mutilated crotch.

"Jesus," breathed a trooper, "it's Mister Rosin!"

A rookie suddenly retched and spewed a sour flood over his shirt.

Dan felt cold sweat work down his sides. The wind fluttered a scrap of paper pinned to the naked chest by a sharp stick.

"The 'Paches are gone," said Haley. "I

scouted up the ridges. Nothing but empty hulls up there." He poured a handful of them on the ground beside Dan. "Forty-four rimfire. Henry rifle ammunition."

Dan nodded. "It figures."

Somewhere over the hills they heard the brassy notes of a C trumpet.

Pale faces rose from behind rocks. A rookie laughed aloud. "Be quiet!" roared Haley.

Dan stood up and leaned on the Henry rifle. "Get a detail ready to cover and load those bodies," he said. "Cut Rosin down."

The trumpet sounded again, closer this time. Dan beckoned to the trumpeter of C Company, a skinny kid not more than eighteen. "Lip onto that trumpet," he said. "Let them know we're alive."

C Company's trumpet rang out brassily, if somewhat shakily.

Three men appeared atop the western ridge. Ducey, Captain Charles Norman and First Lieutenant Miles Danforth of Company B. Dan stood up and waved at them. Norman led his company down the slope in column of fours. Dan walked toward them. Norman reined in. "Hell to pay," he said. His face was serious. "I knew damned well Morris would create trouble. I had no idea how much."

Dan looked back over his shoulder. "Assign Danforth to C temporarily."

"Where are their officers?"

"Rosin is dead. Horace and Kroft are missing."

"For God's sake!"

The troopers of C had wrapped the bodies in blankets, and now lashed them across skittish horses. Haley led a detail to recover the body of little Bertram Morris. It had not been disturbed.

"What are your orders, sir?" asked Norman.

"Send C back to the post. Danforth can look for Horace on the way. We're riding to the reservation."

"Now? With Hair Rope on the warpath?"

Dan eyed the serious officer. "We've got to find Kroft."

A trooper led up Dan's bay. He swung up on the horse. "Haley!" he called, "accompany me as orderly!"

"Yes, sir!"

Danforth formed C Company. He mounted and led them toward Dan. "Your orders, sir?"

"Back to Costain. Keep your eyes peeled. The road is fairly open. You'll only run into an ambush if you get careless. Tell Captain Morgan to send word to headquarters about Morris' death. I'll send a detailed report when I return."

Battered C Company rode up the ridge, many of the troopers riding double. Behind them were the horses carrying the blanketed forms of the dead.

B Company rode up the valley with a point and flankers out. The sun tipped the eastern ranges as they debouched onto a level plain stretching along a branch of San Ignacio Creek. Several miles to the northeast a pall of smoke hung against the fresh morning sky.

Ducey scouted ahead as they neared the reservation. He waved the company on from a low swale overlooking the creek bottoms. The smoke was thick along the edge of the swale.

Dan drew rein on the lip of the swale. Fires smoldered in the ruins of about half a hundred wickiups. There was no sign of life other than a skulking dog which ran off into the brush. On the far side of the creek fires flickered about the foundations of half a dozen buildings. Scattered about the ground were iron bedsteads, pots and pans, smoldering mattresses, shattered boxes and barrels.

"The new buildings Morris was so damned proud of," said Ducey as he cut a chew. "A house each for Cut Lip, Yellow Bear and Long Hat. They didn't use them much. One of Cut Lip's young sons died in his house last year of the coughing sickness. Cut Lip left it and went back to his wickiup."

Dan looked up at the brooding hills. Somewhere in there was Cut Lip's band, now *broncos* as well as those of Hair Rope; warriors, squaws and children. "Mister Kelly," he said to the junior officer of the company, "take a platoon along the bottoms and see what you can find."

"Meaning Mister Kroft, sir?"

"If he's there."

Kelly jingled off with his men. Haley thrust a hand inside his shirt and drew out a scrap of paper, smeared and bloody. "This was struck on Mister Rosin," he said.

Dan read it aloud. "To the White-eyes," it said in misspelt English, "We have closed the door on you. We have gone into the mountains as men and hunters. Do not follow. I have spoken. Hair Rope."

Norman spat. "I didn't know the bloody bastard could write," he said.

Ducey looked up. "His squaw can. She went to the reservation school."

Kelly brought back his platoon. "No sign of Kroft, sir."

"What now?" asked Norman. "Do we go into the hills after them?"

Dan shook his head. "That's what he'd want. Back to Fort Costain."

The column jingled off across the plain. The words of old Black Wind sifted back into Dan's mind. *Listen, Nantan Eclatten! My people are angry. The young men sharpen their arrows and grease their guns.*

They buy fine rifles with the yellow iron which the White-eyes love more than anything else. They have asked my council and I have spoken. I advised peace, but if they do not heed my words your lodges will go up in smoke. Your wagons will be captured. Those of you who wear the blue suits will die in the mountains and deserts. The signal fires will rise from here to Sonora.

B Company received a smoky welcome when it reached Fort Costain. The smoke drifted up thinly from the stables, now nothing but great blackened rectangles on the barren earth. Ellis Morgan was stamping back and forth in headquarters, rawhiding the sergeant of the guard, when Dan came in. He stopped as he saw Dan. "God almighty," he said. "They fired the stables with flaming arrows just before dawn. The wood was dry as old bones. Luckily we got the horses out."

"Who was officer of the guard?"

"Mister Baird. It wasn't his fault. Sergeant Bennett was asleep in the guardhouse instead of making his rounds."

"Confine Mister Baird to quarters. Break Bennett."

Morgan nodded sourly. "What happened at San Ignacio Creek?"

Dan sketched in the details. "Horace and Kroft are missing. Rosin is dead."

"Horace is here."

"Get him!"

An orderly was sent for Horace.

Morgan waved a thick hand. "One word of warning. Horace has friends amongst the high muckymucks. Go easy."

Horace bustled into headquarters. "Thank God you're safe, Major Fayes," he said.

Dan's cold eyes held those of the plump officer. "I see you're safe enough," he said quietly.

Horace flushed. "I was cut off."

"No more than I was."

Horace fiddled with his gunbelt. "The brush was thick with them, sir."

Dan waved a hand. "I'll excuse you for getting cut off. There's no excuse for laxness at San Ignacio, however. Both of your junior officers were gone from your company. You had no sentries out. Rosin was killed and mutilated. Kroft is still missing."

Andrew Horace paled. "It was a complete surprise, sir."

"Damn it, Horace! You've been in this country for some time. You knew the Apaches were restless. Your company was cut to pieces through damned carelessness on your part!"

Horace raised his head angrily. "So? Where were you when the peace commissioner came? It was your duty to take him there. Not *mine!*"

Dan stood up. "You're confined to quarters until further orders."

"General Crook will hear of this!"

Dan smiled grimly. "Certainly he will. Through my report."

Horace stamped out of the office. Dan turned to Morgan. "I'm promoting Haley to sergeant major."

"A deserter? You'll destroy the morale of the squadron!"

"*What* morale? Haley stepped in and held that john company together to keep them from being cut to pieces. Their own noncoms were panic-stricken. Their officers were all gone. Kroft and Rosin looking at squaws. Horace hiding in the brush. Haley is sergeant major. Post it."

Morgan's face went dark with the rush of blood.

"I want a patrol to go into those hills. I want one good officer to lead them. Picked men. Meanwhile clean up the post. You've got materials for new stables. Get the quartermaster busy on them."

Dan walked to his quarters.

Mister Sykes led out a ten-man patrol at noon, guided by Ben Ducey. At three o'clock smoke signals drifted up from the hills. They had been seen.

Gila Barnes came into Dan's quarters in the late afternoon. He squatted near the door and accepted a cigar.

"What did you learn?"

Gila lit up. "The hills are thick with *broncos*. I got as far as Skull Butte before I had to turn back. They've got a camp somewhere in the country behind Skull Butte.

Found a prospector dead in the hills. Apache work."

"Beats me how Hair Rope cut C Company up at San Ignacio, got Cut Lip's band to pull out, and still had time to double back here to fire the stables."

Gila puffed at his long nine. "Hair Rope didn't fire the stables."

"The three top bucks of the band were at San Ignacio. Cut Lip. Yellow Bear. Long Hat."

Gila waved his cigar. "I was comin' out of the hills this mornin'. Saw dust. Ten bucks rode past. You'd never believe who was leadin' them."

"Keep talking."

Gila looked up. "Black Wind."

"Blind?"

"His cayuse was bein' led. There was no other buck of real warrior status with them. I overheard them laughing about burning the stables."

"I wondered where the old coot was."

"Hair Rope is a killer. A real sure enough quill, but he hasn't got the brains to strike like Black Wind can. I'll be willin' to bet the shootin' at San Ignacio was Black Wind's idea."

Dan paced back and forth. "This is a mad business. A blind war chief."

"Not so mad. Black Wind is held in great respect by every Apache between here and Durango. Why, hell'sfire, Dan! He fought with Cochise and Mangus Colorado! He was a great warrior when they were kids! If he stays on the warpath you'll never know what hit yuh!"

Dan smashed a fist into his other palm. "Sykes is leading a patrol into the hills."

Gila nodded. "I met him. Told him to camp high at night. No fires. Ducey is a good man. He'll take care of Sid and his detail."

"This thing has turned into a stinking mess. With a record like this I won't be here long."

"They haven't relieved you yet, have they?"

"No."

"Then forget it."

"Those bucks had Henry rifles, Gila. New ones."

Gila nodded. "So did Black Wind's men."

"Where are they getting them?"

Gila stood up. "I'll mosey down to Moore's and then into Mesquite Wells. Might learn something."

Dan walked to the small hospital and found Myron Cornish wearing his rubber apron. At the rear of the room was the line of dead from San Ignacio. Trooper Felton lay on the operating table in the deep sleep of chloroform. Cornish held out a mutilated slug at the tip of his Blasius pincers. "Forty-four caliber," he said, "Henry cartridge. Half-ounce ball. Felton will live. So will Lowell. Seligman is dead. The slug went into his chest and lodged near the heart. I probed with a Nelaton. Impossible to extract."

The mingled odors of blood, carbolic and chloroform were thick in the stuffy room. Cornish rinsed his hands in the pinkish water of a basin. "Rather interesting mutilations," he said.

Dan looked up. "What do you mean?"

Cornish jerked a thumb at one of the

shrouded figures. "Mister Rosin. A good part of it was done while he was still alive. Rosin had a lot of resistance to live so long."

Dan felt a little sick.

Cornish dried his smooth hands. "They say an expert can keep them alive for hours, almost beyond belief."

Dan eyed the cold man with a little disgust.

Cornish removed his apron and shrugged into his fine uniform blouse. "Still, they say the Moors passed their skill on to the Spaniards. The Spaniards, in turn, taught them to the Indians. Rather interesting, isn't it?"

"Yes," said Dan dryly.

Cornish looked at him with mild amusement. "By the way. Melva would like you for dinner tonight."

"Some other time, Cornish."

The surgeon shrugged. "As you wish. She's all woman, and she likes you, Dan."

"Thanks." Dan left the reeking room and drew deep lungfuls of fresh air into his lungs. Over at the cemetery the burial detail had already started the row of fresh graves.

The sun had gone, staining the western sky with streamers of rose and gold. Dan went to his quarters. Melva Cornish was sitting on his bunk. She stood up as he entered. "Are you all right, Dan?"

"Yes."

She placed a hand at her throat. "I was worried about you."

He looked at her. A faint hunger crept over him. She seemed to be ripe for the taking. "I told your brother I couldn't make it for dinner tonight, Melva."

"That's quite all right. There will be other times."

She came close. "I'm so glad you're all right," she said. Suddenly she held his face in both cool hands and kissed him gently. Then she was gone leaving the imprint of her soft full mouth on his dry lips and the faint intriguing odor of heliotrope.

Dan saw a bottle of mezcal on the table. He uncorked it and drank deeply. There was a weariness in him, not so much of the body, as of the soul.

He lit his candle lantern and drew a chair to his desk. He started his report. His mind mechanically composed the details, as it had so often done before, keeping to the facts, eliminating unnecessary information. When he reached the part where he must write of the raid on the post he put down his pen and took another drink. Who would believe that a *blind* chief, an old man, fit only for long hours of sleep and soft food, could strike as though he were young again? Yet Dan believed Barnes. He compromised by stating that the raid had been led by Black Wind, mentioning nothing of his blindness.

Someone tapped at the outer door.

"Come in!" called Dan.

Surgeon Cornish looked into the room. "I have a list of needed medical supplies, sir."

"Can't the quartermaster take care of them?" There was a faint note of irritation in Dan's voice.

Cornish eyed the bottle on the desk and then shook his head. "Department requires the approval of the post commander."

"Help yourself," said Dan, shoving the bottle and a glass toward Cornish.

Cornish poured three fingers and poised the bottle over another glass. He looked at Dan. Dan shook his head. Cornish shrugged and sipped at the liquor. "Ah," he said, "a man needs this after time in the dispensary."

The faint odor of carbolic seemed always to hover about Cornish, as heliotrope clung about his sister.

"You've done well here, Major Fayes," said Cornish.

Dan rested an elbow on the desk. "I'm glad *someone* thinks so."

Cornish waved a well-scrubbed hand. "You can't be blamed for that trouble at San Ignacio. Horace is a bumbling fool. Morris was so wrapped up in his own importance he never realized the Apaches are humans too. Morgan was always lax with Kroft and Rosin."

"You seem to have formed definite opinions about all the officers here at Costain, Cornish," said Dan dryly.

Cornish smiled. "I'm a scientific man, sir. The field of physical medicine will some day be well supplemented by that of the mind. In Europe there are men who probe the mind as we do bullet wounds. Man is a fascinating study. His foibles and weaknesses; his fears and ambitions. We all have our weaknesses." He looked pointedly at the bottle.

Dan poured a drink.

"You're West Point of course?" asked Cornish.

"Class of 1858."

Cornish refilled his glass. "It seems unusual for a man of your experience and record to be shunted aside to Fort Costain."

"I usually don't question my orders."

Cornish smiled. "Of course not. Yet, you were a colonel at twenty-three. Quite young."

"Volunteers."

"Even so. Still, they kept you on as cavalry inspector, with the rank of major. Very unusual."

Dan sipped his liquor. The man's probing questions and insinuations irritated him.

Cornish lit a cigar. "Let us hope your

record continues. The Apaches are certainly riled up. New rifles. Plenty of ammunition. Good leadership. It will test your mettle . . . and ours, sir."

Dan fingered the requisition Cornish had placed on the desk. "I'll look this over."

Cornish nodded. "The way things look I'll have quite a drain on my supplies."

"I hope not."

Cornish stood up. He paused at the door. "If you have any problems don't hesitate to consult me. Most of us like to talk about our problems. A sort of mental catharsis."

Dan placed his hand over the papers on his desk. "These are my problems at the moment."

"A word of advice, Major Fayes. You're starting to drive yourself too hard. Perhaps you're also lacking the fuel that kept you going during the war."

Dan looked up quickly. "Just what do you mean by that, sir?"

Cornish glanced toward the bottle. "Nothing, sir, nothing at all." He left the quarters.

Dan got up and walked to the outer door

to watch Cornish cross the dark parade-ground. The man rubbed him the wrong way, yet he seemed to have Dan's interest at heart. Dan looked into Dunphy's old room. He lit a lucifer and looked at the dark stain on the floor. What had happened to him? *His* record had been good also. He had had the love of a fine woman like Harriet Moore. Yet the strain had been too much.

Dan went back to his room, looked at the bottle, then stoppered it and put it away. He could feel the little alcohol he had consumed already working within him. The old strain was getting hold of him again.

Mess Call sounded across the dark paradeground. Dan went back to his desk. Food had no interest for him, but the liquor did. He drew his report toward him and set to work, but every now and then he looked at the cabinet in which he had placed the bottle. It was almost as though he could look through the warped wood of the door and see the squat bottle sitting on the shelf.

9

SYKES'S patrol came back the second day after the fight at San Ignacio Creek. Men and officers gathered about the dusty, weary troopers. Three of the troopers were afoot, leading two horses apiece. Three others were in the saddle, bloodstained bandages showing against the dusty blue of their uniforms. Across three horses were limp bundles, troopers swathed in their blankets.

Sykes swung down from his horse and saluted Dan. "We were ambushed near Sand Springs, sir. Three men wounded. Three killed. One missing."

"Where's Ducey?"

Sykes wiped the dust from his haggard face. "He was separated from us."

"Come to my quarters." Dan walked across the sun-beaten paradeground.

Sykes dropped into a chair and accepted a drink. "I'm sorry about the whole thing, sir. Ducey led us into the hills. We watered the horses at the Springs and then climbed up onto a small mesa. I put out double guards, and had the horses on one picket line. The night was quiet. Ducey left before dawn to do some scouting. Just as the first light came we heard the howling of a coyote. It was repeated several times from different places." Sykes lowered his head.

"Go on!"

"They hit us right after that. Kepke and Riordan went down at the first line. The horses almost stampeded. Corporal Clothier and Private Wascher went to quiet them down. That's the last we saw of Clothier. Later we found Wascher gutted at the bottom of the mesa. We holed up. We were in a bad way. Two men wounded. We hardly saw them, yet they covered every inch of ground with rifle fire."

"Repeaters?"

"Yes. Henrys, I think." Sykes drained his glass. "We stayed holed up until the sun rose. The Apaches were gone. I waited for Ducey and Clothier but they never appeared. I came back as quickly as I could."

"Who was leading the Apaches?"

Sykes looked up. His dark eyes held a strange light in them. "I saw an old warrior high on a hill. He looked like a mummy up there, staring at us. Then he was gone."

"Black Wind?"

"I've never seen him, sir. The worst part of it was the laughing when we left the hills."

"The laughing?"

Sykes nodded. "Apaches. Somewhere. We never saw them. It was damned weird, hearing them laugh from the hills, the echoes carrying it along."

Dan eyed the young officer. He seemed to be of good material, yet his nerves were at the straining point. "Get some sleep," he said. "Make out your report when you feel better."

Sykes stood up. "Thank you, sir." He hesitated.

"What is it?"

"When do we get a crack at them, sir?"

"When we're ready. They'd like to have

us come into the hills, bent on revenge, then shoot us up."

"This whittling process hasn't helped the morale any, sir."

Dan looked up. "We'll stop it."

After Sykes left, Dan called for his horse. He rode down to the road and headed for Moore's Ranch. The rancher was in the big barroom. He silently listened as Dan told him the story. "What is it you want from me?" he asked.

"How in God's name are the Apaches getting new Henry rifles?"

Moore leaned on the bar. "It's nothing new. I've known about it for some time. Hair Rope had new repeaters as early as the first of the year, six months ago."

"Perhaps he gets them in Mexico?"

"I doubt it. There are stocks of repeaters in Tucson, and other towns. A merchant can order as many as he likes and doesn't have to account for his sales. I myself have bought them there. I had twenty of them in stock as early as last March."

"How many do you have left?"

Moore looked quickly at Dan. "Ten.

Why?"

"Just curious."

"I sold four of them to miners. Three to people in Mesquite Wells. One to Captain Morgan. One to Captain Norman. I can't remember where I sold the last of the ten." Moore's voice was cold.

Dan lit a cigar. "I didn't mean to imply that you had been selling them to Apaches."

"The only guns I ever sold them were some old Burnside single-shot carbines. That was last summer. Eight of them. I requested authority from the army to make the sale, and received it."

Hoofs clattered on the hard earth in front of the big building. A familiar voice carried to them. It was that of Forrest Kroft. "We'll have a couple of drinks before we return to the post, Gila."

"You're carrying a load now. You want Major Fayes to rawhide you?"

Kroft came into the barroom, followed by Gila. The officer paled as he saw Dan. He swayed a little. "Major Fayes. I'm reporting back to duty, sir."

Dan held back the acid in his voice. "Here? Where have you been?"

Kroft glanced at Gila. "Mister Rosin and I were at the reservation. They shot at us from the brush. Rosin was killed. I managed to get away. I got lost in the hills."

Dan gripped the edge of the bar. "Rosin wasn't killed. He lived long enough to be tortured to death. Who did it, Mister Kroft?"

Kroft looked sullen. His handsome face was flushed with liquor and anger. "I don't know, sir. All I saw were rifle flashes and shadowy figures."

"How long were you in Mesquite Wells?"

Kroft bit his lip. He glanced at Gila. "A few hours."

Gila shifted his chew and looked at Dan.

Dan thrust out a hand toward Kroft. "Sober yourself up before you return to the post. When you do, write out a full report, then stay confined in your quarters."

Kroft saluted.

Jim Moore jerked his head. "There's coffee in the kitchen. The water bucket is just outside the door." He watched Kroft as he walked stiffly into the kitchen.

Dan turned to Gila. "What's the truth?" he asked.

"He was mixed up in a big poker game last night, started a fight and got damned drunk. I found him this mornin'. He asked me not to say anythin'. Hell, Dan, he's rotten clear through."

"Gambling on a shavetail's pay in Mesquite Wells?" asked Moore. "He couldn't have played very long with those sharpers."

Gila shrugged. "He's damned lucky Ace Deming didn't kill him."

Dan poured a drink and handed it to Gila. "Maybe his family has money?"

Gila shook his head. "His father went broke in the panic. He hasn't got a peso comin', outside of his army pay."

A pan clattered on the kitchen floor. There was a scuffle of feet and the sharp outcry of an angry woman. Moore ran to the door followed by Gila and Dan. Harriet Moore stood near the rear door holding a poker in her hand. Her face was flushed and her breasts heaved. Kroft was holding his left shoulder. He turned as Moore closed in on him. "The bitch hit me with that," he said.

Moore's left fist shot out, connecting with Kroft's jaw. He staggered and swung wildly at Moore. The older man thrust out his right arm. The stub smashed against Kroft's mouth, driving him back over a chair. He tried to get up and then lay still. Blood poured from his slack mouth.

"The bastard," said Gila quietly.

Moore turned to Dan. Thin lines etched themselves from the corners of his mouth almost down to his chin. "Get him out of here," he said coldly, "or I'll kill him."

Dan strode to the unconscious officer. He picked up the water bucket and doused Kroft with it. Kroft opened his bloodshot eyes. Dan gripped him by the collar of his shell jacket and pulled him to his feet. He frog-marched him to the front door and shoved him toward his horse. "Damn you," he said thickly, "I'll break you for this."

Kroft dabbled at his smashed mouth.

"She's nothing but a saloon bitch," he said drunkenly.

Dan hit him across the face with open hands. "Get back to the post, you drunken scum," he said.

Kroft swung up on his horse. "You'll pay for this. You and that woman in there. No one hits me and gets away with it." He spurred his sorrel hastily as Dan dropped his hand to his Colt. Dan watched him ride down the slope to the road. He turned in the saddle as he reached the road and shot a look of pure venom at Dan. Then he was gone.

Dan walked into the common room. Moore was filling whisky glasses. "I've had trouble with him before," he said.

Harriet stood in the kitchen doorway. "He's paid for it," she said. "You won't prefer charges against him, will you, Dan?"

"I'll give him a chance to resign."

Gila leaned against the bar. "They won't accept a resignation now, with the 'Paches on the war trail."

Moore tossed down his drink. "He's bothered her before," he said. "Kroft is the type that thinks brass buttons and a commission allow him free rein with any woman. No woman is a lady to him. They're all fair game."

Harriet smoothed her hair. "He's young," she said.

Moore turned angrily. "Not *that* young! He knows better! Keep him out of here, Fayes, or I'll kill him the next time he bothers Harriet."

Dan nodded. "Come on, Gila," he said quietly.

They rode toward the post. "What did you learn?" asked Dan.

Gila shrugged. "Not a hell of a lot. About the rifles, that is. It ain't hard to run in rifles. Any wagon can bring 'em in. The boxes can be marked anything."

"The whole thing is full of holes. Still, my job is to calm down this uprising, not to worry about gunrunners. God knows the *broncos* seem to have enough rifles."

"Yeh. But the more rifles they get the more warriors they can recruit. Bucks just waiting to get their greasy hands on new repeaters." Gila bit off a chew. "Funny thing. Kroft had plenty of gambling funds from what I heard."

Dan looked quickly at him. "So?"

The faded eyes held Dan's. "He was using gold dust until he went broke."

"What are you driving at?"

"Nothin'."

They followed the fort road and passed the gate. "Where is Kroft quartered?" asked Dan.

"In Bedlam."

"Bedlam?"

"Yeh. The junior officers' quarters. At the end of Officers' Row."

"Dormitory?"

Gila shook his head. "They each have separate rooms." He looked at Dan. "You thinkin' the same thing I am?"

Dan nodded. "Can you get in and out of there without being seen?"

"At night mess the place is empty as last night's whisky bottle."

"Go ahead then."

Gila spat a stream of brown juice. "Dunphy had a hell of a time with Kroft.

Kroft seemed to have some hold on him. Dunphy wasn't himself for a long time before he blew out his brains."

"Mister Kroft is quite a man for his age."

Gila nodded. "He likes money, liquor and wimmen. He doesn't get them as a second looie of horse soldiers." Gila rode toward the corrals.

Woodridge, the adjutant, looked up as Dan came into headquarters. "Do you wish to reassign the officers, sir?" he asked.

"Why?"

Woodridge leaned back in his chair. "C Company hasn't an officer left, what with Rosin dead and Horace and Kroft confined to quarters."

Dan dropped into a chair and lit a cigar. "I see what you mean."

"Dennis Halloran reported in. He brought the dispatches from Fort Grant." Woodridge handed them to Dan.

Dan scanned the first two papers. They dealt with supply and transportation subjects. The third dealt with the messy affair at San Ignacio Creek. Dan read it slowly.

From: B. N. Curtiss, *Col.*
Dept. Adjutant, Department of Arizona
Fort Grant, Arizona Terr.

To: Daniel R. Fayes, *Major*
Provisional Squadron, Cavalry
Fort Costain, Ariz. Terr.

Subject: Apache Uprising 5 June 1873

As of this date there are no re-enforcements available for your command. One squadron of cavalry, regularly assigned to this Department, supplemented by three companies of infantry, has been temporarily transferred to the Department of California, for duty against the Modocs in northern California and southern Oregon, thus seriously weakening this command. These are your orders:

1. The murderers of Bertram Morris, peace commissioner, must be arrested and confined at Fort Costain.
2. In an effort to quell the uprising,

you will take the field with your entire command, less one full company for garrison duty, which will remain at Fort Costain.

3. Details of troops will be assigned to duty in Mesquite Wells as per the request of a committee of citizens of that town, as well as any outlying habitations which may require them.

4. All reservation Apaches will be returned under guard to the San Ignacio Reservation. The band of the chief known as Cut Lip will be disarmed and kept under guard until further orders.

5. Upon completion of the above orders you will hold yourself in readiness for travel to Fort Grant for a court of inquiry into the San Ignacio affair. This order includes the presence of A. N. Horace, Captain, US Cavalry.

6. The subject matter contained herein will be strictly complied with as expeditiously as possible and will be held in confidence.

B. N. CURTISS,
Department Adjutant

Dan placed the order on the desk and looked at Woodridge. "You read it?"

"Yes, sir."

Dan rubbed his jaw. "What is the present garrison strength?"

Woodridge took out his Morning Report. "Thirteen officers. One hundred and twenty-eight other ranks. One civilian scout. One civilian interpreter."

Dan shook his head. "With a handful of men I have to garrison Costain—run down Hair Rope and Cut Lip—provide guards for Mesquite Wells and anyone else who feels the need of army protection. No matter which way you figure, we'll be stretched almighty thin, Nat."

Woodridge nodded. "You're damned if you do and damned if you don't."

Dan nodded. "Send word to Horace and Kroft that they are relieved from confinement to quarters. Assign Halloran to C Company. How many men in the guardhouse?"

"Seven."

"Have them released and return them to their companies."

Dan stood up and paced back and forth. He didn't trust C Company in the field. They'd have to stay at Costain as garrison. They had been whittled down to thirty-five men. Horace was of no use in the field, yet Black Wind's raid on the stables, had shown the contempt he had for the garrison of Fort Costain. The Skull Butte country was unknown to Dan. Gila Barnes knew it and so did Ducey, but it was one thing for a few good men led by capable scouts to penetrate into hostile country; it was quite another matter to take a column of morale-rotten troops in there.

"Write out an acknowledgment of that order and send it to Curtiss," said Dan. "Captain Morgan can take his A Company to Mesquite Wells in the morning. He can arrange the details about guarding outlying houses. I'll speak with him about it tonight."

"Yes, sir." Woodridge stood up. "I must say, sir, that I feel a lot better with you in command here."

Dan walked to the door. "Thanks, Woodridge. We've got a tough job of work to do. There will be plenty of empty McClellans before we're through." He walked out of headquarters.

10

DAN dressed slowly for mess. He had no wish to look at the sullen faces of the officers he had released from confinement to quarters. Someone tapped at the outer door as he finished dressing. He started toward the room door and then stopped, glancing at his Colt. The wound on his left shoulder had healed but he had no wish to have a skulking warrior work on him again with a knife.

"It's Cornish, sir!"

"Come in."

Myron Cornish walked smiling into Dan's room. "Melva insists that you come over tonight. How about it? You've turned us down a few times already, sir."

Dan hesitated. It was a sure out from going to the regular mess. "All right, Cornish," he said.

"Fine! Say about eight?"

"That will be fine."

Cornish leaned against the wall. "Rumors are thick about the post," he said. "The sanitary sinks are buzzing with them."

"We have orders to pursue and arrest the Apaches who killed Morris and Rosin."

"The whole squadron?"

"No. C will garrison. A will ride to Mesquite Wells in the morning to guard civilians. I'll have to take B."

Cornish studied his neat nails. "What happens to me?"

"Have you a capable man or two to use as medical orderlies?"

Cornish nodded. "Sergeant French is a good man. Orderly Andersen has a great deal of experience."

"Andersen can go with A Company to Mesquite Wells. You can stay here with C or go along with the field column, whichever you prefer."

"I have some supplies coming in which I'd like to check."

"Then French can go with the field column."

"Fine. I'll help him prepare his panniers."

"How are Orskin, Mehaffey and Rinke?"

"Orskin and Mehaffey are all right. Rinke has a trace of blood poisoning. That's another reason I'd like to stay at the post. Rinke may lose his arm. Arrow wound."

Dan eyed the surgeon. "They used *arrows*?"

"Yes. I extracted a sagittate flint head from the wound. Poisoned, I think. You know how they make their poison?"

"No."

Cornish smiled. "Very interesting. They place a fresh deer liver on an anthill and let the ants fill it with their venom. The big Sonoran ants. When the liver is filled with it they let it rot and then dry, making a powder of it which they mix with a little grease. This is daubed onto the arrowhead. Gangrene is usually the result if the wound isn't taken care of in time."

"Very interesting. But why would they use arrows when they have Henry rifles?"

The dark eyes studied Dan. "Fear, I suppose."

"What do you mean?"

Cornish waved a hand. "The whole post knows Rinke was wounded with an arrow. If gangrene *does* set in and he loses his arm, the thought of what happened to him will remain in the minds of the troopers who chase the Apaches. Psychology, Major."

Dan nodded. "Very efficient."

"They are. A remarkable people, the Apaches. I've heard it said that they know of hidden lodes of gold. Wealth that would turn any white man's head. Yet they rarely use it."

"You'd think they'd use it instead of waiting for government handouts."

Cornish eyed the glasses on Dan's desk.

"Drink?" asked Dan.

"If you'll join me."

Dan poured two drinks and handed a glass to the surgeon. Cornish eyed the liquid and then downed it. "Speaking of handouts. Actually the reason they are so bitter against the government isn't that they really need handouts, as you call them, but rather because they feel that the government made them promises, and to an Apache, you must keep your word. It's as simple as that."

"I wish it was as simple to get them back on the reservation."

Cornish nodded. "By the way, Forrest Kroft is very bitter toward you. A very angry young man. Watch yourself, sir."

"What do you mean?"

Cornish smiled. "Kroft is unstable. He feels as though you destroyed his dignity. A bad place to hit a man."

When Cornish had gone Dan refilled his glass. Cornish was as smooth as silk, with his perpetual smile and insinuating talk. There was no real reason for Dan to dislike him, yet he was glad to see the surgeon leave.

It was eight o'clock by Dan's repeater watch when he walked down to Cornish's quarters midway down Officers' Row. The adobe was set farther back from the row line, overlooking the creek bottoms, placed on an outthrust point of ground with deep gullies on either side of it. Dan made a mental note that the gullies should be either filled or banked, for a heavy rain would eat away the earth dangerously close to the walls of the adobe.

Yellow lamplight showed between the trim curtains of the windows. Dan tapped on the door. It was opened by Melva Cornish. She wore a low-cut gown exposing the deep cleft between her full breasts which seemed to strain against the dress fabric. She held out a slim hand and gripped Dan's. "Just in time," she said. "Would you like a drink before dinner?"

"Yes."

Dan felt a fullness in him as she brushed past to lead the way into the snug living room. She spoke over her shoulder. "Wine? Brandy? Whisky?"

"Wine will be all right." The mezcal Dan had taken aboard had filled him with a comfortable warmness. He sat down in a big chair. Melva had done wonders with the poor quarters. Navajo rugs covered the packed-earth floor. A trim Argand lamp shed soft light from a marble-topped table.

On the walls hung several oils of local scenery. Melva saw Dan look at them. "Some of my work," she said.

"You have talent, Melva."

She flushed a little. "Myron says so. It keeps me occupied in this lonely place."

She placed the glass on the table beside his chair. "I'm so glad you could come, Dan." She sat down and leaned back in her chair. "We'll dine in a few minutes."

Dan glanced at the table, covered with a heavy damask cloth. It was set for two. A smaller lamp brought out the highlights of the heavy polished silver. "Where is Myron?" he asked.

She leaned forward. The lamplight brought out the color of her firm breasts. "Didn't he tell you? Oh, that absent-minded man! He went into Mesquite Wells, to consult with Doctor Walsh about poor Trooper Rinke's wound."

Dan nodded, as he sipped the wine. It was very cozy being alone with Melva Cornish. A commander who dealt with men all day needed a woman to come home to, even at a place like Fort Costain.

She eyed him. "I hope you're not disappointed."

"No."

"I know how you men like to talk business."

"I'm a little tired of business now, Melva."

He drained his glass and she rose to fill it. The fragrance of her body and heavy perfume worked on him as the liquor did. Suddenly he felt completely weary of his profession.

They dined quietly. Melva was a skillful cook and a polished hostess. Dan found himself growing more interested in her. She still reminded him strongly of Kitty St. Clair in Washington, but there was a difference. Kitty had been easy to understand. In most ways, she was almost as simple as a man, while Melva had all the intrigue and challenge of her sex.

When they left the table, Dan sat in the big armchair and looked about the room. It would be fine to have quarters like this. Quite different from the monk's cell he lived in. On the mantelpiece sat some rock samples. Melva followed his glance. "Myron collects them while in the field."

"A man of many interests."

She laughed. "Yes. *He's* never lonely, Dan." She smoothed her thick hair. "What with his medicine and rock collecting he's quite contented."

"I often wonder why a doctor would enter the service. Low pay. Rough assignments. Little chance to get ahead in the profession."

The dark eyes flicked at him and then away. "There are times when I wonder about Myron myself. Before he went to medical school he talked of nothing else. At school he astounded his professors with his quick grasp of any subject. After his internship in New York, in the tenement areas, he had a chance to go to Europe to study at Edinburgh, but he turned it down."

Dan sipped his wine. "I wonder why?"

She clasped her fine hands together. "I'm not sure. Sometimes I think it was because he worked so hard to go to medical school, depriving himself of everything but the bare necessities. . . ."

"So he became an army surgeon for a pittance when he could be well paid for his services anywhere else."

She leaned her head back against her chair. "Why did you become a soldier?" she asked.

He grinned. *"Touché!"*

"I mean it. Why?"

"My father was a soldier. Both of my grandfathers were soldiers."

"So it was the thing to do."

He shook his head and refilled his wineglass. "No. I would never have gone to West Point unless I had believed implicity that I wanted to be a soldier."

"Then you might try to understand Myron."

"There's a difference. A soldier doesn't serve for pay. There are other things."

"Glory? Prestige?"

"In a way. There's more than that. It is a way of life to which one is committed."

She arose and paced back and forth, the odor of her perfume reaching tempting fingers out to Dan as she passed near him.

Something about the comfortable room was also bothering his mind. The furnishings were expensive. The silverware on the table had cost a pretty penny. Yet she had said Cornish had deprived himself of everything but the bare necessities to gain his education. Money spoke in a metallic voice in that room, so different from other contract surgeons' quarters he had visited throughout the West.

She stopped beside his chair and looked down at him. Dan stood up and reached out a hand. She placed her warm one in it and Dan drew her close. He met no resistance. She raised her full lips to his. He crushed her soft body close and felt her smooth arms slip about his neck and draw him toward her, straining her body against his. His eager hands explored her upper body, the liquor he had consumed fueling the hot fire within him. They swayed a little as they experienced each other's lips and bodies.

She broke away and touched her hair. There was a strange look in her dark eyes. "I should never have let you come here to be alone with me," she said huskily.

He reached for her. "Why?"

"You know how talk gets around on a small post."

"I'm worried!"

She backed away from him. "It's getting late, Dan. Please! Some other time."

He closed in on her and drew her close. She struggled a little and then sought his lips eagerly. He drew her toward the couch and pulled her down beside him. It had been a long time since he had held such a woman in his arms.

Boots grated on the hard earth outside the quarters. She jerked upright. "Get away from me," she said.

"It's just some trooper."

She shook her head. "We're too far back from the other adobes for anyone to be walking around here."

"It's the guard," he said desperately.

She stood up and walked to the table. She picked up the decanter and filled his glass. Dan shrugged and walked to his chair. She stood looking down at him. "There is plenty of time in the future," she said.

He drank half of his wine. "Perhaps. I'll

be leaving for the field very soon."

"You'll be back, Dan."

"Possibly. It's a dirty business, Melva."

Something brushed against the outer wall. She tilted her head. "You hear?"

Dan stood up. Every fiber in him cried out to take her now, completely. He picked up his forage cap. She was right. There would be plenty of time. "Good night, Melva."

"Good night, Dan."

She came to him as he reached the door and kissed him softly and then she was gone.

Dan shrugged. He opened the outer door and felt the cool night air rush about him. The moon hung in a cloudless sky. There was no one in sight. He walked slowly toward his quarters, feeling for a cigar. He stopped in front of the building and lit up. He drew the smoke deep into his lungs. Suddenly he had to fight down the desire to get his horse and ride into Mesquite Wells.

Dan opened the outer door of his quarters. Something moved at the far end of the hall. Instinctively he dropped to the floor.

A spurt of flame reached out from the darkness. The roar of the gun was deafening in the low hallway. Then the rear door opened. He saw a shadowy figure against the light for a moment and then the door banged shut. He jumped to his feet and dashed out the front door. Feet grated on the hard earth behind the quarters. He ripped his derringer free from his pocket and ran around the adobe.

Something moved beyond the washhouse. He snapped out a shot and heard a muffled exclamation. A pistol flared again and the slug slapped into the adobe inches from Dan's head. Shards of hard clay splattered against his face. Tears flooded his eyes. He ran toward the washhouse. His assailant would have to slide down the eroded escarpment behind it.

A man yelled from the guardhouse, followed by the steady pound of feet as the guard raced from the building.

Dan stopped beside the washhouse, and looked down toward the creek bottoms. The area was bathed in silver moonlight, the shadows of the mesquite and cactus sharp on the pale earth. Nothing moved.

Dan turned as the corporal of the guard pounded up followed by four men. "Get down into the bottoms," he said. "It's only one man."

"Apache, sir?"

"Damned if I know! Get moving!"

The corporal plunged down the slope followed by his men. They spread out into a line and worked toward the silvered loops of the shallow creek. Dan walked back toward the paradeground. Ellis Morgan trotted toward him, breathing heavily. "What the hell is going on?"

"Someone waited in the hall for me. Shot at me. I got one shot in."

"Apache?"

Dan waved a hand. "I don't know. He was wearing boots."

"Some Apaches do."

Dan became irritated. "All right, all right. So they do. I *said* I didn't know who it was."

Morgan flushed. "I'll turn out my company to scour the bottoms."

"No. You're leaving for Mesquite Wells

in the morning. Let the men get their rest."

Morgan wiped the sweat from his face. "I'd like to speak with you about that."

"Go ahead."

"I'm senior company commander. It seems to me that my company is getting the wrong assignment."

"It does? Why?"

"Hell, Major! I think I should stay here and command the post in your absence. Certainly Horace hasn't got the ability to do it."

Dan raised his head. "It seems to me I was sent here to command this post, Captain Morgan. Are you questioning my authority?"

Morgan cut a thick hand sideways. "No."

"Then do as you're ordered. By God, I never saw a command like this. Every damned officer seems to think I'm riding him."

Morgan closed a big fist. He lowered his head. Almost as though planning to charge Dan. Then he looked down and saw the moonlight glinting on the silver-chased derringer. Slowly he raised his head and opened his fist. "Woodridge told me to report to you earlier this evening. I couldn't find you."

"I was dining at the Cornishes."

The dark eyes half-closed. "Myron is in town," he said.

"So?"

"You were alone with Melva?"

Dan slipped the derringer into his pocket. "Yes."

Morgan stared at Dan. "I hope you enjoyed yourself."

Dan came closer to Morgan. "Get the hell back to your quarters, Morgan! Another thing: Don't ever question my orders again!"

Morgan turned and strode off across the moonlit parade-ground, slamming his heels hard against the earth. Dan watched him until he disappeared into the shadows at the far side of the post. He felt for a cigar and lit it. The big man was jealous. Damned jealous . . . and dangerous.

The corporal of the guard panted up the

steep slope. "No sign of anyone down there, sir."

Dan nodded. "Take your men back to the guardhouse."

He walked into his quarters and lit the candle lantern. He drank deeply and stripped off his clothing. As he closed his eyes to sleep he thought of the warm voluptuous body of Melva Cornish. She was ripe for the taking but it would take time. A *little* time.

11

THE squadron officers were assembled in headquarters the morning after Dan's narrow escape. Dan leaned against the wall. "Read Curtiss' order," he said to Woodridge. Woodridge read in a clear strong voice.

Dan studied each man as Woodridge plowed through the order. Baird and Sykes of Company A seemed to be fairly reliable. Captain Norman of B was solid and unimaginative. Danforth and Kelly, his junior officers, were run-of-the-mill, although Kelly seemed to show some promise if he was handled right. They would be all right with Norman. Horace was a damned weak link in the chain and Dan had his doubts about his remaining in command at Costain, but Dan didn't trust him in the field. Kroft leaned against the wall, slowly turning his forage cap in his hands. He looked away sullenly as Dan glanced at him. His face was still bruised. Dennis Halloran, the first lieutenant who had returned from the hospital at Fort Grant, was a lean man with the Antrim look about him. He seemed to enjoy the admiration and respect of all the post personnel. He would fortify the weaknesses of Horace's command. Collier Crispin, the Q.M., was a scholarly officer, small and efficient with serious blue eyes behind his glasses.

Myron Cornish straddled a chair in a corner of the big room. He smiled as Dan looked at him. Thoughts of what he had learned from Melva about her brother ran through Dan's mind. He wondered what Melva had told *him* about Dan.

Woodridge finished the order and looked expectantly at Dan. Dan stood up. "You may smoke, gentlemen." He lit a cigar as some of them got out their smokes. Cornish slowly tamped tobacco into a fine English briar.

Dan took his cigar from his mouth. "In that order we have the bare essentials of what we must do. Any questions?"

Morgan looked up. "Paragraph Two

clearly states that you are to take your entire command, less one company for garrison duty, into the field, sir. Yet your orders are for my company to go to Mesquite Wells for guard duty, leaving you but one company."

Dan nodded. "Paragraph Three states that details of troops will also guard Mesquite Wells and vicinity. I don't see how it can be done with less than a company."

Morgan shrugged.

Dan puffed at his cigar. "I'm making one change. Mister Kroft will accompany B Company as junior officer."

Horace jerked his head. "I'll need him, sir!"

"You have Mister Halloran. There will be two other officers available should you need them. Mister Collier and Mister Woodridge. Surgeon Cornish will remain here as well."

Kroft glanced angrily at Cornish.

"There's no need to tell you gentlemen that we're stretching things pretty fine," said Dan. "Horace, I want double guards every night."

"The men will be tired."

Dan waved a hand. "You can eliminate all unnecessary details. The men can get plenty of bunk fatigue. Horace." He paced back and forth. "Morgan, I don't want you to spread your men too thinly. Keep two squads in Mesquite Wells. The citizens there have guns. If any attack is imminent you can declare martial law and draft the citizens to help you. Detail a few men at each outlying house or ranch that requests them. Keep patrols, under competent non-coms, in the hills about the town."

"Yes, sir."

"That is all for Companies A and C. Morgan, you will move out as quickly as possible. Take enough escort wagons for your extra equipment and food. How many will you need?"

"At least four, sir."

Collier stood up. "We've only six on the post, sir. Six others were destroyed in the fire. That will leave only two for you, sir."

"We're not taking any where we're going. We'll use pack mules."

The officers of A and C saluted and left. Dan sat down and puffed at his cigar.

"There's no need to tell you officers what we face out in the hills. Gila Barnes will scout for us. Sergeant Andersen will go along as medic. His panniers are prepared, Cornish?"

"They're always ready, sir. I checked them this morning."

"Good. The head of B Company will pass through the gates at dusk."

"Why so late, sir?" asked Norman.

"There are probably Apache eyes watching this fort at this very minute. I don't want them to know we're leaving."

"Fine, sir."

"Full field equipment. Three hundred rounds of carbine ammunition per man. Fifty rounds per revolving pistol. Rations and forage for seven days. Officers' Call will be at 5:30 P.M. Co-ordinate your watches." Dan took out his watch and snapped open the case lid. "It is now 10:45 A.M. Officers may take repeating rifles if they have them. Any questions, gentlemen?"

Kroft raised his head. "I don't feel too well, sir."

Dan held the red-rimmed eyes with his.

"Did you report for Sick Call, Mister Kroft?"

"No, sir."

Dan looked at Cornish. "Examine him after dismissal." Second Lieutenant George Kelly, who stood beside Kroft, moved a little way from him. Tall Miles Danforth could hardly hide the disgust on his lean face.

"Dismissed, gentlemen!" said Dan. He watched them file from the room.

Woodridge spoke up. "Will you take Sergeant Major Haley, sir?"

"Can you spare him?"

"Yes. Linke is a good man. He can take over."

"Then Haley will go."

Woodbridge grinned. "It would have broken his black Irish heart if he couldn't have gone. I feel rather badly myself about not going. Any chance, sir?"

Dan shook his head.

"I could take Kroft's place, sir."

"That young man is going to sweat. I'll dry the alcohol from his system. We'll make a sharp command out of this john squadron, Woodridge."

"I have no doubt about that, sir."

Dan was in his quarters when Gila Barnes came into the room.

"Did you check Kroft's quarters?"

Gila nodded. He thrust two fingers into the right-hand pocket of his worn coat. He brought out a small packet of paper and placed it unfolded on the desk. Gold dust glittered in the light that came through a side window.

"Where did you find it?"

Gila helped himself to a drink. "In the pocket of a pair of his trousers. There was a little more in a shirt pocket."

Their eyes met above the desk. "I think I'll take a ride into Mesquite Wells this afternoon," said Dan quietly.

Before Dan left the post after noon mess, Cornish had sent his orderly to tell him that Kroft was fit for field duty.

Mesquite Wells dozed in the afternoon sun. Here and there, amongst the false-fronted wooden buildings of the American period, were thick-walled adobes of the earlier Mexican period. The hills hung over the town. Smoke drifted up from the mine buildings on the rugged slopes. Here and there the tailings from the mines erupted like great swollen scars, covering brush and earth.

Dan passed a peeled-pole corral at the edge of town and saw the bays of A Company there, under guard of two men. He dismounted in front of the marshal's office and went in. A thick-bodied man, wearing a star, stood up as he entered. "Can I help you, Major?" he asked. "I'm Ben Forepaugh, city marshal."

Dan nodded. "Major Dan Fayes, commanding officer of Fort Costain. I'd like to ask you a few questions in strictest confidence."

Forepaugh accepted a cigar from Dan. "Glad to be of help, sir. Damned glad you sent some of your men here to help out in case the Apaches attack. What can I do for you?"

Dan lit up. "I've a young shavetail on the post. A Mister Kroft."

Forepaugh's head snapped up. "Forrest Kroft. What do you want to know?"

"Something about his gambling."

"He's done a lot of it in the last six months or so."

"So I understand. Seems odd. A second lieutenant's pay won't stake a man very much."

Forepaugh's gray eyes held Dan's. "I've often wondered about it myself. Unless Kroft has been out prospecting, which I doubt, it does seem odd he should have gold dust to gamble with."

"I understand he was in here a couple of days ago."

Forepaugh nodded. "He was in a game with Ace Deming. Kroft claims Deming cheated. Deming almost drew on him."

"So?"

"Ace Deming is an honest gambler. Slick as goosegrease but no one has ever questioned his honesty. Kroft is damned lucky he didn't get killed." Forepaugh eyed Dan. "Just what are you driving at, Major Fayes?"

"The Apaches have been getting Henry

rifles regularly since the first of the year. I've heard they pay gold dust for them."

Forepaugh took his cigar from his mouth. "I can't believe it. An army officer! If you can't trust army officers out here, who *can* you trust?"

"*One* army officer, Ben."

Forepaugh nodded. "I'm sorry. Still, I don't think Kroft has the brains to work a gunrunning deal."

"Neither do I. But he may be fooling us. I'd like to talk with Deming if he'll keep his mouth shut."

"He will. He's my half-brother, Fayes. I'll get him right away."

Forepaugh came back with a slim man, dressed in sober black, his face freshly shaven but still showing the dark shadows of a thick beard on the smooth cheeks. He nodded as Dan was introduced. "How can I help you, sir?" he asked.

Dan spoke about Kroft.

Deming lit a cigarillo. "Up until three months ago Kroft always gambled with hard cash. Plenty of it and no dust. One night he got liquored up and ran out of cash. His credit stinks here in town. He was so damned mad he brought out a poke of dust. I didn't question it. Why should I? Gambling is my business; not Pinkerton work."

"How much would you say Kroft has shown in the last three months?"

Deming relit his cigarillo and eyed Dan over the flare of the block match. "Close to two thousand dollars, I'd say roughly."

"Damned near two years' pay."

Deming nodded.

Dan paced back and forth. "Keep your mouths shut about this."

Deming waved a slim hand.

Dan leaned on Forepaugh's desk. "What's your opinion on this gunrunning, Ben?"

"It would be easy enough to get away with. Buy guns in Tucson. Freight 'em up here. Run a wagonload out into the hills and bargain with the Apaches. They pay two or three hundred in dust for them."

"Anyone else use gold dust in town?"

"A few prospectors. The miners are paid in cash. As far as I know none of the men that pay their way with dust can be suspected. I may be wrong."

"Keep a record of them, if you will."

The gray eyes studied Dan. "And the officers?"

Dan nodded. "*And* the officers."

Deming looked up. "I'll help too, Major. I learn a lot across the green cloth."

"I'd appreciate it." Dan walked to the door.

Forepaugh stood up. "Jim Moore does most of the freighting around here, Fayes," he said.

Dan turned. "So?"

"It'd be damned easy for him to run in guns."

A cold feeling came over Dan.

"Just a thought, Fayes," said Forepaugh.

Dan pushed open the thick front door of Moore's Ranch. The common room was empty. Someone moved in the kitchen. He walked to the door and looked in. Harriet Moore was taking some freshly baked pies from the oven. The heat had flushed her oval face. She carried a pie to the table and brushed back a wisp of hair.

"You seem to fit in a kitchen," said Dan softly.

She whirled. "You gave me a start," she said.

He leaned against the side of the door. "I'd like a piece of that pie, Harriet."

She pulled out a chair. "Sit down. There's fresh coffee. When do you leave?"

"After dusk." Dan eyed her as he sat down. She seemed very cool toward him.

She cut the pie and poured coffee for him. "I wish you luck," she said. "Surgeon Cornish told us last night that we'd be safe enough here."

"Behind these walls? I have no doubt about it."

She nodded. "We can take care of ourselves."

He started on the pie. "You're quite a cook, Harriet."

"Dad thinks so."

"Where is he?"

"In the barn checking out a new shipment."

He finished the pie. She offered no conversation as she worked. Dan lit a cigar and refilled his coffee cup. "You're still angry about Forrest Kroft?" he ventured.

She shrugged slim shoulders. "Why should I be? He learned a lesson. I've forgotten him."

"You seem put out with me then."

She looked at his plate. "Would you like more pie?"

He smiled. "I'd like one to take along. Seven or eight days of field rations are rough on a man."

"I'll give you three. One for Sergeant Haley. You can give the other to your officers."

"That will include Mister Kroft."

"I don't begrudge any man on patrol a piece of pie, Dan."

He rested an arm on the back of his chair. "This is rather silly, isn't it?"

"I don't understand."

"Talking about pie . . . and Mister Kroft."

Her eyes held his. "What would you like to talk about?"

"I'd like to visit you when we return from patrol."

"The bar is always open, Dan."

"I'm not interested in the bar, Harriet."

"So?"

"I want to see you."

"I'll be here," she said coolly.

He got up and walked to her. "What's wrong, Harriet?" He took one of her hands but she drew it away. "The least you could do is tell me what is wrong."

She looked up into his face. "It would be better if you stayed on the post and visited Melva Cornish," she said quickly.

"Well I'll be damned! Begging your pardon, Miss Moore."

She walked to the rear door. "I must help Father now." She left the kitchen.

Dan walked out behind her. Jim Moore was standing at the tailgate of a freight wagon in front of the big barn. Harriet took the freight bill from his hand. "I'll finish this, Dad," she said. "There's pie and coffee in the kitchen."

Dan walked with Moore into the kitchen. "Harriet seems put out with me, Jim."

"So?" Moore cut a piece of pie and poured coffee.

"What's wrong?"

Moore sat down. "Myron Cornish was here last night. He mentioned the fact that you were dining alone with Melva."

"He was supposed to be there. I didn't know he was gone until I got there."

"I believe you."

There was something in his tone that caused Dan to look closely at him. "By God, Jim! I'm getting tired of this run-around. What's bothering Harriet?"

"Harriet likes you, Dan. A great deal. More than I had realized. She liked Jim Dunphy. I won't say she loved him. Jim was a good man but damned weak. I suppose it's the maternal instinct in women that makes them that way. My wife was like that. Harriet has a lot of Agnes in her."

Dan relit his cigar. "Keep talking, Jim."

Moore loosened his collar. "Melva Cornish set her cap for Jim Dunphy. Jim wanted nothing to do with her, but Melva is a strong-minded woman. She practically threw herself at him. She gave Harriet a hard time one night at a squadron dance at the post. Made remarks about a saloon-keeper's daughter. Harriet is too much of a lady to fight back. Things went from bad to worse. Dunphy drank a hell of a lot more. Then one night he went over the deep end and was found the next morning dead, with his service pistol in his hand. Harriet took it very hard. It didn't seem to bother Melva Cornish. She started after Ellis Morgan. It seems as though she must hold the affections of the post commander at Fort Costain. She can do it too."

Dan nodded. "She's all woman."

Moore looked up. "Myron Cornish laid it on damned thick last night, Dan. He seemed to gloat over the fact that Melva had an in with you."

"Melva Cornish has no hold on me."

Moore stood up. "Remember one thing. If she does interest you, I want you to stay away from Harriet. I don't want her hurt again." There was a quiet warning in Moore's tone.

"I won't hurt her, Jim."

"See that you don't!"

Moore followed Dan to the outer door. "Be careful," he said. "You've got a john squadron under you. I think you can whip them into shape. But no cavalry company carrying cookstoves can track down Hair Rope and Black Wind."

Dan mounted Hardtack and looked down at the one-armed veteran. "Say good-bye for me to Harriet, Jim."

Moore nodded. He watched Dan ride down the slope. His eyes were cold as ice. Then he smashed a big fist against the door and went inside.

12

B COMPANY was butt-sprung and crotch-weary after four days on the trail. Dust coated the blue uniforms a neutral color and thickened the speech of the tired troopers. The hills about them were dim in haze. There was no sign of life. There hadn't been in the four days of the patrol. No smoke against the sky. No skulking *broncos*. Yet fear rode knee to knee with most of the men of Company B. There was nothing but the empty miles behind them and the unknown miles ahead. There was an aura about the slowly moving company with its tail of dusty mules. Sour sweat, the nitrogen odor of horses, dust and damp leather.

Dan looked from beneath the brim of his hat at a lone speck far ahead on a long slope. It was Gila Barnes, riding his ewe-necked roan in tight little circles. *Something* was up ahead at last. Dan thrust up an arm and heard the column come to a jingling, stamping halt. The dust swirled up about him. A mule bawled from the rear of the column where Mister Kroft cursed luridly as his long-eared charges milled about, trying to rub their packs off against each other.

"What is it, Dan?" asked Captain Norman.

Dan shrugged. He eased a dirty finger beneath his sweat-soaked collar and lifted the soggy cloth away from his sun-scoured neck. "Sergeant Haley!" he called out.

Haley spurred his big bay forward and saluted.

"Come with me," said Dan. "Charlie! Ten minutes rest for the company. Loosen girths. Check those goddamned mules. Kroft is off in one of his tantrums again."

Haley took a chew from his pocket. "Ready for some Wedding Cake, sir?"

Dan grinned. "Strong, but the sauce is good. Is that it, Haley?"

Up ahead Gila had stopped circling his roan. He hunched in his battered Mexican saddle, like a gnome.

When they drew rein beside him, the

scout jerked a thumb toward the steep slope behind him. "Look," he said laconically.

Wheel tracks showed in the loose sand at the bottom of a shallow wash. "So?" asked Dan.

Gila shifted in his worn saddle. "I was up the wash. There's been a camp there. Recently. A white man. Wagon. Four mules drew wagon. Yuh'd better take a look-see, Dan."

"What the hell for?" demanded Haley. "What's wrong with a waggin bein' out here?"

Gila looked at Haley with ill-concealed disgust. "With no roads? Thirty miles from nowhere?"

"Gila, you stink."

"You're no Rose of Tralee, you ugly bastard."

They grinned at each other as Dan rode down the slope to follow the wagon tracks. The wash curved and a grove of smoke trees showed huddled against a rough wall of rock. Dan slid from his saddle at the sight of a circle of ashes on the earth.

Gila led up his roan. "Look," he said. He

picked some partially burned pieces of wood from the fire. They were packing cases. He crossed to a hollow and picked up an object. It looked like a small mat of hair. He handed it to Dan. "Scalp," he said. "White man's." He felt about beneath a bush and brought up a small pot. It had been covered with cloth which had been tightly stretched and bound about the pot with strips of rawhide. There was a small hooped stick at his feet. "'Pache water drum," said Gila. He picked up the hooped stick. "Beating stick."

Dan squatted in the shade of a smoke tree and looked at Gila. "Keep talking, Gila."

Gila shifted his chew. "There was a dance here. The ground has been tromped plenty. Apaches don't treasure scalps like other tribes. Use 'em for one dance and then throw them away. The medicine is gone outa them after the dance."

"What about the wagon?"

Gila nodded. "There was a white man here. Boot marks in with the moccasin tracks. Broken whisky bottles all over. Quite a baile they had." He walked to the fire and held out a piece of partially burned wood. "Take a look at this."

Dan examined the wood. It had been stenciled. "Dried Fish." The other side was greasy to the touch.

Gila jerked a thumb toward the smoke trees. "Over there are a bunch of broken cases. All marked 'Dried Fish'. You note the grease on the wood?"

Dan nodded.

"That there is gun grease."

Dan rubbed it between his fingers and held it to his nose. He nodded.

"Damned queer," said Gila. "Dried fish cases with gun grease in 'em."

Haley eyed the gaunt scout. "So they had dried fish," he said.

"Yuh ain't got the brains yuh was born with, Haley, Dan knows what I'm drivin' at."

Dan threw the wood down. "Apaches won't touch fish, Haley. It's taboo. No one knows why. The reason is buried somewhere in their mythology."

"It's nice to have an education," said Gila dryly.

Dan spat out his chew and reached for a long nine. He lit it and eyed Gila through the bluish smoke. "Anything else, Gila?"

Gila thrust a dirty claw into a pocket and brought out half a dozen Henry rimfire hulls. "Found these scattered up the wash, Dan."

Haley rubbed the reddish bristles on his jaw and looked at Dan. Dan tossed the hulls up and down in his hands. "Some white man brought guns in here, thirty miles from nowhere, packed in cases labeled 'Dried Fish'. He met the *broncos* here. There was a scalp dance. Some of the bucks tried out their new guns and left the hulls."

"Keno," said Gila.

"The question is: Who was the white man? We know too damned well who the *broncos* were."

Gila stood up. He pointed north. "Look."

A thin raveling of smoke etched itself against the clear sky, miles away.

"Haley," said Dan, "bring up the company. Where's the nearest water, Gila?"

"There's some *tinajas* two miles up the

wash. Usually got water this time of year. Yuh kin bivouac up on a rock slope from there. Fairly safe position."

Haley swung up into his saddle and spurred his bay back down the wash.

Gila leaned on his long Spencer rifle. "How'd yuh like to take a walk with me tonight, Dan?"

"Toward the smoke?"

"Yes."

Dan relit his cigar. "You've read my mind, Gila."

"That ain't easy."

The company was bivouacked for the night on a rocky slope, the horses picketed against a wall of rock. The troopers lit no fires after dusk. A soft velvety darkness covered the low mesa which loomed behind them. Beyond the bivouac area a circle of troopers lay behind their saddles, fingering their carbines, listening, hardly daring to breathe for fear of not hearing.

Dan followed Gila through the darkness. The scout moved like a ghost, trailing an aura of tobacco smoke, sweat and greasy leather. Dan moved silently but clumsily in his spurless, cloth-wrapped boots. The wind whispered through the darkness, rustling the ocotillo and mesquite, mumbling strange thoughts to Dan. They had covered at least three miles since leaving the horses several miles from the bivouac area.

Beyond them the dim shape of the mountains showed blackly in the darkness. A coyote howled plaintively from the mesa.

Gila stopped. Dan halted just behind him. The scout seemed to be testing the night with all his senses. He spoke over his shoulder. "Smell it?"

Dan was about to say no when he caught the odor of bitter smoke, faint and tantalizing. "Apaches?" he asked.

Gila shook his head. "Not this low. The bastards camp high. The one thing they fear is surprise."

"White men then."

"Probably. *Quien sabe?*"

Gila leaned his long Spencer against a rock. "Stay here." He vanished into the darkness like an ill-smelling phantom.

Dan squatted beside a rock, fingering his Winchester. He hungered for a smoke and then remembered that Haley had given him a cut of Wedding Cake. He placed the chew in his mouth and worked it into pliability. He grinned as he thought of his last year in Washington. He wondered what some of his society drinking companions would think of him now, squatting in an Arizona gully, stinking enough to enrage his own sense of smell, chewing a wad of spit-or-drown. He needed a shave. He itched. His feet, socks and boots were larded together. *I'm crummy*, he thought, *lice-bitten and stinking, but I'm doing the job for which I was trained, and to hell with Washington society.*

The whipsaw scream of an eagle floated down to Dan from the dark mass of the mountain ahead of him. Far off to the right was the macabre bulk of Skull Butte, crannied and eroded, shrouded with brush, the top of a great granite dome. Like a decayed skull with some of the dry hair still clinging to it, two shallow caves marking the hollow eyes, a gully marking the nose hole and a rock ledge forming the slitted mouth. All the days of the patrol they had seen it, aloof and lonely, seemingly watching their snail-like progress across the desert and into the barren hills.

Dan scratched a dank armpit. The company had shaken down quite a bit. The recruits had learned to handle themselves in the field while the veterans had lost their garrison softness. He shifted his chew and spat into the darkness. In the final analysis it would be the showdown with the Apaches that would prove whether or not B Company was fit to call themselves US Cavalrymen. It was one of the worries that gnawed at Dan's mind like a hungry rat.

The soft hoot of an owl came to Dan. He stiffened and then relaxed. An Apache wouldn't use the hoot of an owl for a signal, for Bu, the owl, was a harbinger of ill luck.

Gila seemed to swim up out of the darkness. He knelt beside Dan. "Camp up ahead. At a *tinaja*. One man. Four mules and a mountain waggin. He's asleep in the waggin."

Dan stood up. "Any sign of Apaches?"

Gila shook his head. "Shall we take him?"

"I want to question him."

"Go easy then. A man's liable to be jumpy out here at night."

Dan spat. "Why? He can't be worried. Camping here with a fire in hostile country."

They padded off into the darkness. The smell of smoke came strongly to them as the wind shifted.

Gila stopped in a thicket and held up a hand. Dan looked down into a wide hollow, thick with scrub trees and brush, dim and indistinct. Now and then the fire flared up from the bed of embers encircled by blackened rocks. Beyond the fire was the dim outline of the wagon. A mule stamped its hoof.

Gila eased down the slope. Dan squatted beside him. They scanned the area for long minutes, listening and sniffing. Gila nodded. Dan placed his ear close to Gila's ear. "Circle around. When you're ready, hoot like an owl. I'll close in. No shooting."

"Keno." Gila slipped into the enveloping night.

The owl hoot drifted across the hollow. Dan eased his Colt out of its holster and padded down the slope. He circled the fire. The wagon was covered with a ragged tilt. The side toward the fire was rolled part way up, but the interior was too dark for him to distinguish anything. Dan approached the wagon. One of the mules bawled. One of his mates picked up the tune. Something moved in the wagon.

Dan stopped by the seat. The man in the wagon cursed softly. He bumped the side-board as he thrust a long leg over the side toward Dan. Gila appeared near the tail-gate. The man dropped to the ground and reached inside the wagon for something. Gila moved like a cat. The man turned. He was taller than Dan by a head. Gila closed in, striking out with his pistol. The man evaded the blow. Dan jumped forward. Gila was smashed against the wagon.

The man turned as Dan came in. He fended off the blow of the Colt and drove in a jolting blow to the jaw. Dan bounced off the wheel, his senses reeling. Gila drove a shoulder against the man. He went down. As Gila closed in he was met by a long pair of legs. The socked feet drove into Gila's gut. The scout's breath went out of him in a gush.

Dan ran in again, smashing with the Colt. It was knocked out of his hand. He evaded a lashing blow, sank a left into the lean gut and followed through with a right hook. His opponent grunted in pain. He snatched up a stob of wood and threw it at Dan. It glanced from his shoulder as he charged in. Long arms reached out, gripped Dan by the shirt front and pulled him forward to meet a downthrust head. The skull crashed against Dan's chin. He brought a knee up hard into the groin, clasped both hands together and smashed them down on the back of the neck.

The man went down to meet an upthrust knee. He grunted in agony and rolled over toward the fire.

Blood dripped from Dan's chin as he pulled the tall man away from the hot embers. His clothing had already started to smolder. Dan squatted and scratched a lucifer on his belt buckle. He stared at the battered face. "Jesus," he said softly.

Gila spat. The juice slapped into the dust with the sound of a dropped pack of playing cards. "Ben Ducey."

Ducey moaned a little as he opened his eyes. "Who is it?" he asked.

"Major Fayes. Gila Barnes," said Dan quietly.

Ducey sat up. "What the hell kind of game is this?"

"That's what we'd like to know," said Dan.

Ducey tenderly touched his battered face. "You're a good man for the rough-and-tumble, Fayes," he said.

"Thanks. You're good yourself. Now start talking."

"What do you want to know?"

"Plenty. What happened to you after Sykes's patrol was ambushed?"

"I was cut off in the hills."

"Where'd you get the wagon?"

Ducey spat out some blood. "I always had it."

"What are you doing out here?"

"Looking around."

Gila looked at Dan. "Right out in the middle of nowhere with a waggin and four mules. How come yuh didn't ride a hoss or a mule, Ben?"

"A man can travel any way he wants."

Gila nodded. "Carrying what?"

Ducey stood up. "You can look in the waggin."

"We won't find what we want in there, Ben."

Ducey eyed Gila. "What *are* you looking for?"

"Henry rifles," said Dan quietly.

"I got a Sharps."

"I said *rifles*."

Ducey threw back his head and laughed. "You don't imagine I'd be gunrunning, do you?"

Gila leaned against the wagon. "Funny man," he said.

"Take a look in the wagon, Gila," said Dan. He cocked his Colt. "Now, Ducey. You've been missing quite some time. We find you out here with a wagon. There's no town or ranch within miles. The Apaches are raising hell. This has a damned queer look."

Ducey yawned. "I got tired of interpreting and scouting. Got too rough. Damned if I mind going out with experienced troops, but these john companies you have will only get cut up like Sykes was. A man has to look out for his future."

Gila poked his head beneath the tilt. "I'll bet you are," he said. "Not much in here, Dan. Blankets. Some food. Sharps rifle and a Remington pistol. No freight."

Gila slid from the wagon. "Seems as though someone had a waggin farther south, along a wash. Seems as though somebody was carrying dried fish."

"What's wrong with that?"

Gila spat. "Dried fish packed in *gun grease*?"

"You've been eating peyote."

Gila shook his head. "Tastes like dirt. Never could stand the stuff. I'll stick to forty-rod."

The wind fanned the fire. Dan studied the lean face of the interpreter. Ducey's eyes shifted. "There was a scalp dance down the wash," said Dan. "Somebody was firing Henry rifles. We found the empty hulls. There were boot tracks mixed up in the moccasin tracks. Come clean, Ducey."

"I don't know what you're talking about."

Dan looked at Gila. "Search him."

Gila worked swiftly through Ducey's clothing. "Pipe. Tobacco canteen. Matches. Coupla pistol cartridges. Wallet. Loose change."

"Look around that wagon."

"He's been in there," said Ben Ducey.

"*In* there," said Dan. "I'm thinking of the rest of the wagon."

Ducey fingered his lower lip, watching Gila from beneath drawn brows.

Gila crawled beneath the wagon. "Water bucket," he said, "Tar bucket." He opened the toolbox ironed to the side of the wagon. He lit a match and poked about in it. "Jack. Hatchet. Nails. Auger. Rope. Linchpin. Kingbolt. Some strap iron." Suddenly he stopped and lit another match. He lifted out a can. "Grease," he said.

The fire flared up. Something glittered on the side of the greasy can. Dan took it from Gila's hands. He held it close to the fire. Flecks of gold dust showed just beneath the rim of the lid. he took the lid off and poked through the grease. Some of the grease came out in a thick ball. The bottom of the grease was caked with gold dust. The can was filled at least half an inch deep with the precious ore. "What's this?" asked Dan quietly.

"You can see! Gold dust."

"Yes, I know. But where did you get it?"

Ducey grinned. "Prospecting. I carry it in there for safekeeping."

Gila scratched his scrawny neck. "Get your boots on," he said.

"You've got no right to arrest me!"

"We'll worry about that later," said Dan. "What happened to Corporal Clothier?"

"How should I know?"

"He went missing at Sand Springs."

"Too bad!"

Ducey pulled on his boots. He lit a cigar and watched his two arrestors. "You'll get yourself in trouble," he said. "I've got friends in this country."

"Yeh," said Gila, "*Apache* friends."

"You've got nothing on me."

Gila grinned. "No? Mebbe you was carrying dried fish to sell to them."

"It's possible. God knows they don't get enough food from the Bureau."

"You've been an interpreter for quite some time," said Dan. "Too bad you didn't spend a little more time studying Apache customs as well as their language. Or you'd know they won't touch fish or animals associated with water."

Ducey glanced nervously at Gila.

Gila shifted his chew and spat leisurely. "Yeh. Anyways they wouldn't touch food packed in gun grease. They ain't *that* hungry!"

Gila hitched up the team. Dan put out the fire. They led the mules up the draw back toward where the horses had been picketed. Ducey walked easily, sucking at his cigar. Dan knew they didn't have a hell of a lot on the interpreter, unless they tied in some other evidence. Ducey wouldn't break easily. The evidence was all circumstantial. The source of the gold dust was unknown. The fact that Ducey had cached it in the grease can meant nothing.

Dan looked back over his shoulder. The moon was pale in the sky, hardly showing enough light to see anything. Somewhere behind them the *broncos* were gloating over their fine weapons. They had magazines that held fifteen rounds, enough to blast hell out of a cavalry unit armed with single-shot carbines. The one advantage the cavalry had was their marksmanship. Few Indians had the patience to practice shooting. Yet Dan knew that his squadron was woefully inefficient in shooting for record. The scales were swinging down for the *broncos*.

13

B COMPANY cooked their bacon and brewed their issue coffee. The thin smoke of the fires hung low in the early morning sky. Dan squatted beside a rock with Captain Charlie Norman. "We've really nothing on Ducey as yet," he said.

Norman swallowed his food and sipped his coffee. "You think he's alone in this deal?"

"No." Dan put down his plate. "I've reason to believe we might blow the top from this thing before long. I've had my eye on someone for a little while."

"So? Who?"

"I'll tell you when I learn more."

Norman stood up. "What are your orders?"

Dan looked at the mountains. "I'd like to probe farther into those mountains but I'm getting worried. We'll swing back around

Skull Butte and head for the upper San Ignacio. If Hair Rope has any idea of hitting Mesquite Wells we may cut him off."

"Supposing he's already been there?"

"I doubt it. No Apache in his right mind would buck up against a cavalry company behind 'dobe walls. Besides, the civilians in Mesquite Wells are not exactly soft touches. The combined fire power of a cavalry company and a score of straight-shooting civilians."

"I'll agree to that." Norman strode down the slope to where his noncoms were eating.

Dan felt for a cigar. Suddenly he raised his head. Corporal Ferris had been assigned to guard Ben Ducey. The noncom was filling his plate at a cook fire. Dan dropped his own plate and hurried over. "Who's guarding Ducey?" he asked.

Ferris smiled. "He's all right, sir. The officer of the guard told me to come and eat."

"Who's officer of the guard?"

"Mister Kroft, sir."

Dan threw away his cigar and walked swiftly through the brush to where Ducey's wagon sat beneath an overhanging rock wall. There was a quick movement in the brush. Forrest Kroft moved across an open space. He whirled as Dan appeared. Then he plunged into the brush. Dan ran after him. Boots grated on the hard earth. Ben Ducey emerged running from the brush, looking back over his shoulder. Dan freed his Colt from its holster. "Kroft!" he yelled.

Ducey slammed his feet down hard. Kroft whipped out his Colt. He raised it as though on the pistol range.

"Kroft!" yelled Dan. "Don't shoot!"

The revolver shot punctuated Dan's order. Smoke drifted back over Kroft. Dan cursed as he plunged down into a hollow. Ben Ducey lay on his face. His long fingers dug into the ground. He jerked spasmodically and then stiffened. Blood soaked through the back of his huck shirt.

Dan knelt by the side of the interpreter and turned him over. His eyes were open.

Troopers yelled in the camp. Captain Norman plunged through the brush followed by half a dozen troopers. Forrest

Kroft slipped a cartridge into his Colt and holstered the weapon.

Dan looked up at Norman. "Dead," he said.

Kroft walked to them. "He made a break for it," he said easily. "I yelled at him to stop. I didn't mean to kill him. I wanted to wing him."

Dan stood up. "Bury him," he said to Norman.

Kroft looked down at the man he had killed. "I feel terrible about this," he said.

Dan held out his hand. "Give me that pistol. You're under arrest."

Kroft shrugged. He handed Dan the Colt.

Dan and Charles Norman walked behind Kroft as he returned to the bivouac area.

"There goes our lead, Charlie."

"Funny thing. Kroft could have winged him."

"How so?"

"Kroft has won many a squadron pistol-shooting match. I've seen few men as good as he is with a handgun."

Dan eyed the young officer. If there was

any connection between him and Ducey there was no way of proving it now. "Boots and saddles as soon as Ducey is buried," he said.

The company pulled out at eight o'clock. Ducey's grave was left to its lonely place. One of the troopers had fashioned a crude cross which stood out above the rocks piled over the grave.

It was late in the afternoon when the company reached the San Ignacio. The point dipped down into a hollow heading for a draw which led down into the bottoms. Something cracked in the brush atop a rock formation. A trooper of the point threw up his arms and slid from the saddle. The point scattered for cover. Then rifle fire broke out behind the company. Slugs whipped into the small column of mules. Norman roared out his orders. The troopers slid to the ground. The horseholders led their charges into a hollow. Carbine fire ripped out, but there was nothing to shoot at but thin wisps of smoke in the thick brush overhead.

Dan squatted behind a rock. The sun

beat down on the rocky earth. Now and then a shot broke the quiet, swiftly answered by the crackle of carbine fire. Three troopers were down. One dead and two wounded. Yet they had seen nothing of the *broncos* beyond the rifle smoke. Charlie Norman crawled to Dan. "What now?"

Dan took his cigar from his mouth. "There can't be more than a dozen or so of them."

"Yes. But we can't get across the open ground to root them out."

"I don't want you to."

Norman wiped the sweat from his broad face. "I figure this way, Dan. They were watching us. They had orders to slow us or stop us near the San Ignacio. Why? Because there's something going on up ahead they don't want us to find out about."

"This trail leads to Mesquite Wells."

Norman raised his head. "You don't suppose?"

"What else?"

"It's loco. They can't take Mesquite Wells."

Dan rubbed his jaw. So far his command

hadn't done much to compete with Hair Rope.

Gila squirmed through the brush. "They pulled foot," he said. "'Bout ten of them ridin' north through a draw. Long Hat was leadin' 'em."

"You"re sure they pulled out?"

Gila nodded. "Just saw 'em. See? The dust?"

Dust rose beyond a low ridge.

Dan stood up. "Send a squad up there, Norman. Gila will go with them. I want that ridge combed."

The company waited in the solid heat. Now and then the sun flashed on metal as the squad moved through the thick brush. Then Gila stood up on a rock and waved his arms in the All Clear.

B Company moved out, taking with them the two wounded troopers. Trooper Archer lay beneath the earth to one side of the lonely ridge. The sun was low now, barely clearing the western ranges. Dan looked back at the lone grave. Suddenly he felt like a damned fool or a green shavetail on his first patrol. The *broncos* had all the cards.

The days of the patrol had not netted Dan one arrest, nor one dead Apache.

The stench of burnt flesh hung thickly in the valley of the San Ignacio, mingled with the odor of burning wood and hot metal. Norman had halted the head of his company on a rise looking down on the Mesquite Wells road. Spaced equally apart were five glowing beds of coals, fanned into flaring life by the night wind which crept down from the ridges. Here and there were huddled figures. Something hung against a wagon wheel which had fallen back against the burned wood and iron of a freight wagon.

Dan jerked his head at Norman. "Stay here. Gila!"

The scout kneed his roan next to Hardtack.

"Come with me," said Dan. "I want a squad, Charlie."

The squad followed Dan and Gila down toward the burned wagons. They rode slowly into the heavy hot air. Wisps of smoke rose up from the wagon ruins.

"Seven men," said Gila.

"Never had much of a chance," said Sergeant Bostwick.

"It stinks," said a trooper.

"What did you expect?" asked Trooper Lane, hatchet-faced and lean. "Oh dee colognee?"

"I'm sick."

"Dismount and puke," said Bostwick. He looked at Dan. "It hits 'em hard the first time, sir."

They dismounted. The green trooper hurried into the shadows. They could hear his retching as they walked about the area. Gila eyed a stripped body. The right shoulder was reddened by the recoil of the rifle. "Put up a fight," he said. "Guess it didn't last long."

The ground was littered with yards of cloth from bolts. Glass crunched underfoot as they walked about. "Whisky," said Bostwick, "cases of the stuff."

"Some drunk," a trooper said. "No wonder they cut up them bodies."

An Apache uses a knife like an extension of his arm, swiftly and without mercy. The honed blades of the *besh* had had their fill of hot blood. Empty cartridge cases littered the torn earth.

Gila stopped beside Dan. "Take a look at this," he said. He walked to the burned and maimed carcass lying on top of the metal of the wagon wheel. Dan eyed the big corpse. The right arm was missing from the elbow down. "Jim Moore," said Gila.

There was a sour taste in the back of Dan's throat. He fought it off and turned away. "Maybe this was why we were held up back at the creek, Gila."

Gila nodded. "Probably had an ambush ready and knew we were in the area. Gave them just enough time to finish the job." He toed a smashed bottle. "By God, they must be plannin' a time tonight up in them hills."

"I feel like a john recruit," said Dan. "They hit and vanish."

Gila cut a chew and stowed it in his mouth. "They sure ain't doin' anything to increase your military reputation, Dan. You're losin face. Fast."

Dan looked south. Somewhere down

there Harriet Moore was in her kitchen, preparing a hot meal for Jim Moore and his teamsters. He'd have to tell her. It was his job. A terrible hunger for liquor swept over him. He needed his glass crutch again.

"Bostwick!" said Dan. "Get the company down here."

The company filed down into the massacre area. Norman dismounted and came to Dan. "Now we know," he said.

"Bury them," said Dan, "This was Jim Moore's outfit, Charlie. That's him on the wheel."

"Good God!"

Dan walked away. He left the burned area and took off his hat. His foot struck something on the ground. A bottle. He picked it up. It was untouched. He worked the cork out and raised the bottle. Suddenly he threw it with all his strength into the brush. A trooper looked curiously at him as he walked past carrying a shovel.

Spades and shovels thudded against the earth. The bodies were rolled in blankets and placed in a neat row. Dan smashed a dirty fist into his other palm. He paced back and forth alongside the shallow creek. There was a coldness in him now. A dark anger against the men who had supplied the *broncos* with repeaters.

Dan felt for his cigar case. His fingers touched the brass reservation plate Black Wind had cast so contemptuously into the road at Dan's feet. He fingered the smooth metal. *Take it! Keep it! Remember it! For you shall not rest by day or night!*

The bitter voice seemed to live again in the night wind. *There will come a time when you shall want to speak with me. Use that plate to the pass through my warriors, before you choose the way of your dying.*

Dan looked up at the dark sky. "Maybe you'll die, Black Wind," he said aloud, "and there will be no way for *you* to choose *your* way of dying!"

Harriet Moore's eyes were dry as she listened to Dan's story of her father's death. She sat at the kitchen table with her slim hands clasped together. When he had finished she bowed her head.

The clock ticked steadily. Dan turned his

dusty hat around in his hands, wishing he were anywhere else, yet wanting to be with her.

She looked up. "Thank you, Dan," she said quietly.

"Is there anything I can do?"

She shook her head.

He hesitated. "Have you enough money, Harriet?"

"My father was a wealthy man, Dan. I don't need anything." She stood up and paced back and forth. 'I wanted him to retire but it wasn't in his heart."

"What will you do?"

She shrugged. "Stay here, I suppose."

"It will be a rough job for a woman."

"Yes. But it will keep me busy. I have no other place to go, Dan." She bent her head. "Why did it have to happen?"

"What was he hauling?"

"Liquor. General supplies. Two wagon-loads for Pastor's General Store in Mesquite Wells."

"Any rifles or ammunition?"

She glanced quickly at him and then went to a desk. She took some papers from a drawer and ruffled through them. "Two cases of Henry rifle ammunition. One case of .44's. One case of .45's. One case of .50's." She scanned another sheet. "Ten Henry rifles."

Dan nodded. "Who knew what he was carrying? Beyond your father and yourself?"

"The teamsters, I suppose. The distributor who orders for us." She looked at the last sheet. "There were also some medical supplies for your post. Quite a lot in fact."

Dan walked to her and looked at the sheet. They were items listed which he remembered from Cornish's requisition. Medical alcohol. He knew where *that* had gone. Various medicines. Lint. Retractors. Glassware. "Funny thing," he said, almost to himself, "I saw none of these items in the area."

She shrugged. "Apaches are like children. They'll take anything which strikes their fancy."

Dan nodded. "Will you be all right?"

"Yes. There are four employees here."

"I'll detail a guard."

"Is it necessary?"

"Yes. I feel as though I'm responsible for your safety."

"Do as you think best." She looked up at him. "Will you take me to the grave when you have time?"

"Certainly." He touched her face. "I'll have him brought here for burial if you like."

She shook her head. "Let him stay with his men."

Dan left the building. The dust from the passage of his command hung low on the road farther south. He mounted Hardtack and rode slowly toward the fort. Captain Morgan was damned flustered when Dan asked him why he had allowed Moore on the road without a proper escort. Morgan claimed he had not known Moore was with his wagons. Mesquite Wells had not been bothered. Dan ordered out a strong patrol to search the San Ignacio Valley for possible raiders. It was all he could do.

Dan sat up late in his quarters the night of his return. A pile of orders, requisitions and other military work lay on his desk. He lit a cigar and read again the report which had come in from Department Headquarters. All hell had broken loose in Dan's absence. Three teamsters had been killed on the Union road. A prospector had been tortured to death near Little Wash. A cavalry patrol from Camp Hayes had been ambushed and cut to pieces. Two ranches in the Green Mesa area had been gutted and their occupants massacred. A mining camp near Bitter Water had been besieged, all the horses and mules driven off, and some of the outbuildings burned to the ground. Dan stood up and looked at the map which hung on his wall. He circled each of the points mentioned in the report. He drew a pencil line from the fight which had involved the Camp Hayes patrol, through each of the circled area. It covered a great arc from thirty miles west of Fort Costain, up through the hills, close to Union, then down past the San Ignacio, through the Skull Butte area to Bitter Water, far to the southeast of Fort Costain. All of this had happened in the days of Dan's search for

Hair Rope and his *broncos*.

Dan sat down and lit a cigar. He would need at least a brigade to patrol all those square miles. Gila had told him that Hair Rope had never had more than twenty bucks in his band. Add forty more from the San Ignacio band. That would give Hair Rope a total of about sixty braves. Figuring each war party would number at least twenty to thirty men, it seemed an impossibility for Hair Rope to do what he had done.

Dan eyed the map. The center of the wide radius was north of Skull Butte. That area was malpais. Cut-up land, a jumble of rugged mesas, peaks and hills, in which a cavalry unit could easily get lost, surrounded and smashed. There was no chance for re-enforcements. He had to handle his job with the troops he already had.

Dan took the brass reservation plate from his pocket and looked at it. Cooke's *Cavalry Tactics* didn't cover the situation. The *broncos* had the advantage of knowing the country like the palms of their greasy hands. When they needed horses they stole them. They could live off a country, where even a veteran frontier trooper would have starved to death. Water was a problem for anyone in that country, but the Apaches had the long hard training of doing with as little water as possible. They'd never face a cavalry unit in a knock-down-drag-'em-out fight. It wasn't their way. Strike when the odds were with you. Avoid a head-on clash. Hit hard and then vanish. Guerrilla fighting at its best. That was the Apache way of war.

Dan leaned back in his chair. Gila knew the area where the *broncos* were hidden better than most men and even he admitted that it was a matter of less ignorance of the country, than a real knowledge of it.

"No trooper, carrying a cookstove, can ever catch an Apache in his own country," Dan said aloud. Some of the hard-earned lessons of '59 and '60 came slowly back to him. It wasn't really cavalry country. It was brutally rough on horses. The enemy used horses to get from place to place with incredible speed, made their ambush, fought on foot, then used their horses to get the hell out of the reprisal area. If a horse was run to death a warrior wouldn't be charged one hundred and thirty-two dollars and fifty cents for it. A warrior could get more mileage out of a horse than any trooper. They had ways. If the horse died they cut off the best meat and left him for the buzzards.

The whole damned setup in Arizona was wrong. No Apache chief would have a chance against Jeb Stuart or Phil Sheridan in a *civilized* cavalry encounter. Dan half-closed his eyes. He thought back on the great cavalry commanders of all time. Genghis Khan. Prince Rupert. Murat. Light-Horse Harry Lee. Tarleton. None of their lessons applied here. They might work against Kiowa, Comanche or Sioux with some success, but never against The People. Hair Rope had the advantage that he had made the White-eyes lose face. He would press that advantage to the limit. Every psychological factor was working with him.

Dan got up and paced back and forth. His one advantage was in the white man's ability to outthink the savage. But how? *Break loose from the past* he thought. Think of *something* where your one advantage will even up the odds.

There was a light tap on the door. Dan picked up his Colt. "Who is it?"

"Gila."

"Come in."

Gila dropped into a chair, shoving back his sloppy Kossuth hat. He eyed the map. "Courier just came in from Fort Grant. Good news. In a way."

Dan poured two drinks. "Good news?"

Gila accepted his drink. "Hair Rope was killed two days ago in the Galiuros. Him and five warriors. They raided the corals and was driven off. They headed west and run plumb into a strong patrol. Never had a chance. Cut Lip was captured."

They looked at each other over their glasses. "You're thinking the same thing I am, Gila?" asked Dan.

The scout nodded. "Who in hell's name has been raising the devil in this area?"

Dan downed his drink. "Hair Rope a good eighty miles from here. Cut Lip with him. Long Hat held us back at the San Ignacio while Moore was cut down. That leaves Yellow Bear."

Gila spat into the fireplace. "He's got the mind of an idiot. More interested in squaws than fightin'. He's a *diyi*, anyways, a medicineman, and ain't supposed to fight."

"So who's leading the *broncos?*"

Gila eyed Dan. "One man. Black Wind!"

"Impossible! He's old! He's blind!"

"Yeh. *But who else is there?*"

Dan refilled the glasses. "My God! A pack of *broncos* ripping the country apart, led by a blind chief."

"It's loco. But it's true."

Dan placed a hand on the map covering the area behind Skull Butte. "What do you think the odds are of us getting in there?"

"Jeeesus! Fiddle-footed troopers crashing through the brush in boots. Blind as bats. We'd be wiped out."

"Exactly. That's what Black Wind expects."

"So?"

Dan straddled a chair, resting his arms on the back. "Our trouble is just as you say.

Mounted men trying to track down guerrillas that can outmaneuver us easily. We're limited too much. Now supposing we hand-picked our men. Veterans. The best shots. Got into the hills without being seen by traveling at night. Left our horses and went in on foot."

"You'd have to get rid of those damned stovepipe cavalry boots."

"Make rawhide moccasins."

"The light is dawning."

Dan spoke swiftly. "I'll get repeaters. Enough to go around. If I have to buy them myself. Take the best men from each company. Travel lightly. Do you get it?"

"You're wrecking history, Dan. It just ain't in regulations!"

Dan grinned. "Listen, you hairy-eared bastard! It isn't really new. The British formed light infantry companies in the 1750's, while fighting against the French and Indians. They were trained in scouting and skirmishing. Moved about quickly and quietly. Hand-picked men who could use their own initiative. It was a high honour to be picked for this type of duty."

"What did it prove?"
"That white man *can* use Indian tactics."
Gila pulled at his lower lip. "Waal, it's worth a try, Danny. What do you want me to do?"
"Make a sketch map of the area north of Skull Butte. As well as you know it."
"Keno."
"Meanwhile I'll pick out the men and get the repeaters."
Gila helped himself to a drink. "You'll either make a damned hero out of yourself or end up getting courtmartialed . . . providin' yuh don't get killed."

14

DAN stood at the edge of the parade-ground looking down at the firing range. Sergeant Major Haley was at work with the picked men of Dan's new organization. It hadn't been to well received by Captains Ellis Morgan and Andrew Horace. It was usual army practice to get rid of the misfits and curdle-heads on a new organization. Horace had blustered and Morgan had grown sullen when they saw their best men drawn from their companies to get quartered with the picked men of B Company.

The shining new Henry rifles flashed on the range. A relay was firing. The crackling reports echoed from the low hills and the bluish smoke drifted upward. The shiny brass hulls were ejected from the magazine rifles to clatter on the hard earth. Dan had secured some from Harriet Moore, others in Mesquite Wells, while the remainder had been found at the fort.

Dan lit a long nine. Gila was at work with Corporal Kemper, who had been a shoemaker in civilian life. The two of them were making up knee-length rawhide moccasins, soled with tough leather. Two pairs for each of the forty men of Dan's organization. Farrier-Corporal Brogan was fitting rawhide boots to the picked horses of the command. There was another detail to be taken care of. Dan wanted a medic. Medical-Sergeant French was a good man, skilled in his line, with ten years' frontier service behind him.

Dan opened the dispensary door. French jumped to his feet from behind his desk. "Sit down, French," said Dan. "Is Surgeon Cornish here?"

"No, sir. He went down to Moore's Ranch."

Dan sat down. "How'd you like to join my scouts, French?"

French grinned. "Can I, sir?"

"I'd like to have you if Surgeon Cornish can spare you."

"My medical orderly is a good man, sir.

Used to be a medical student before he took to liquor. He can fill in for me any time."

"Good. Then if Cornish agrees we'll assign you to the scouts."

French nodded.

"By the way, Sergeant. Tell Surgeon Cornish his medical supplies were lost in the attack on Moore's wagon train. He'll have to make out another requisition."

French looked at Dan. "Medical supplies, sir? We didn't requisition any."

"There were medical supplies in Moore's wagons. Alcohol. Various drugs and medical supplies. Lint. Retractors. Glassware."

French tilted his head to one side. "We've got five gallons of alcohol in stores, sir. All the lint we'll need for months. We order retractors about once a year. I know that we don't need any glassware."

"Look up the copy of that requisition."

French looked through his files. He turned to Dan. "The last requisition we made was two months ago. One hospital bed. Two bedpans. Two scalpels. That was all."

"You must be mistaken."

French shook his head. "No, sir. There's no copy here, nor did Captain Cornish mention it to me."

Dan puffed at his cigar. "I see. Tell Captain Cornish I'd like to see him when he comes back." Dan stood up and walked to the door.

French spoke up. "I don't like to get Captain Cornish in trouble, sir, but this happened twice before. Once when Major Dunphy was in command. Later when Captain Morgan took over."

Dan turned. "Speak up!"

"Is that an order, Major Fayes?"

"It is!"

French rubbed his jaw. "I got hell from Major Dunphy at the time. Captain Morgan didn't bother about it when he was in command."

"Well?"

"Both times the supplies came in. In large boxes. Captain Cornish took charge of them. The first time I was out with a patrol and heard about it from the orderly. The second time I received the shipment and Captain Cornish took charge of them too. I never did see what was in the boxes.'

"Keep talking."

"Well, sir. I never saw any new stores in the storage room. Whatever was in those boxes was never put in there."

The rattle of firearms came from the range. Dan looked across the paradeground toward Cornish's quarters. Melva was seated beneath the ramada. "Did you make a report on it to Lieutenant Collier?"

"No. Captain Cornish told me not to bother anyone about it."

"Seems like a hell of a lot of medical supplies for a post that hasn't done much field duty until lately."

"Yes, sir."

Dan turned. "Keep your mouth shut about this, French."

"I will, sir."

Dan walked across the paradeground. There had been a contract surgeon in his brigade of volunteers who had always ordered excessive amounts of alcohol for his own use. There had been a quartermaster officer in a camp along the Rapidan who had done a thriving business in selling issue supplies until he had been caught. Cornish lived well. Far too well for the pay of a surgeon.

Dan sent Booth for Hardtack. When the orderly returned Dan ordered him to clean up Dunphy's old quarters. Dan rode down from the mesa. It was a beautiful day but the sun was hot as the hinges of hell's own door. It would be worse in the hills when he led his scouts after Black Wind.

Cornish's mare was standing hipshot in front of Moore's big building. Dan walked into the common room. Cornish was at the bar idly swilling liquor around in a glass. He turned as Dan entered. "Just in time for a drink, Major Fayes," he said.

"I'm on duty, Cornish."

Cornish smiled. "Here?"

Dan nodded and leaned against the bar. "I want to talk with you about those medical supplies you recently ordered."

"That's why I came down here. Moore was freighting them in. I thought some of the items might be salvaged."

Dan felt for a cigar. Cornish knew there had been nothing salvageable from the burned wagons. The secretive eyes held Dan's for a moment and then looked away.

Dan puffed at his cigar. "It seems as though there is no record of that requisition in your files, Cornish."

"French is careless. I'll speak to him about it."

"It also seems as though some of the items you ordered were not needed."

"For instance?"

"Alcohol. Five gallons are already in your stores. Lint. You've all you'll need for months. Retractors. It seems as plenty. I ordered Sergeant French to tell me about it."

"Have you taken over the surgeon's duties, Fayes?"

There was an impulse in Dan to smash the smooth face before him.

Cornish sipped his liquor. "Another thing: Department Headquarters requires the signature of post commanders on all requisitions. It seems as though you neglected that little detail, sir."

Dan flushed. The surgeon was right. He had told Woodbridge to OK it.

"I suggest that you find those duplicates, Captain Cornish."

"I'll try."

"There is such a thing as the Inspector General Department, Cornish. I wouldn't like to inform them of this carelessness."

"Whose? Yours or mine?"

"Dammit! Watch how you address me, sir!"

Cornish flushed. A tiny muscle worked in his jaw. "Listen, Fayes! You're a career man. I am not. I'm fed up with duty out here. My contract ends in a few weeks. I don't have to renew it. Congress is contemplating the reduction of the Medical Corps, as badly as it needs expansion. I can leave the service easily. Such is not your case. Your record was shaky before you came here. It hasn't gained any luster since. A mess in the requisitioning of supplies wouldn't help you any."

"I see," said Dan quietly. "How did *you* know about my record since the war?"

Cornish smiled. "I have friends in Washington. Some information was passed on to me."

Dan almost lashed out at the smooth smiling face. He controlled himself. "Get back to the post," he said. "You and I will settle this later."

"Any time, Fayes. I always did like a good battle."

The surgeon walked out of the common room. Dan heard the steady beat of his horse's hoofs on the hard road. He took the cigar from his mouth and dropped it on the sanded floor. He ground it savagely beneath a boot.

Harriet came into the room. "I didn't know you were here, Dan."

He took off his hat. "I wanted to see Cornish."

"A strange man."

"I understand he was asking about his medical supplies."

She raised her brows. "No. He wanted to buy the place. He knows it's a gold mine."

"Are you planning to sell it?"

"I don't want to. For a time at least."

"Why?"

She looked steadily at him. "Do I have to tell you, Dan?"

He took one of her hands in his. "I had hoped a little," he said quietly.

She raised her face to his. "Now you know."

He drew her close and kissed her. She placed her head against his chest. "Do you think me bold?" she asked.

He held her close and pressed his lips against her hair. "I'm a fool," he said.

She shook her head. "I didn't know about it until Captain Cornish told me you had been with Melva. Then I was jealous. I fought it off but it was no use."

"Why did you fight it, Harriet?"

She looked up at him. "I lost Jim Dunphy," she said. "Now I know I never really loved him."

He kissed her, feeling the softness of her slim body. It was something wonderful; something he had never hoped for.

"You will be careful, Dan?" she asked. "I couldn't bear to lose you too."

"I'll be all right."

"I hope so. Cornish hates you. Morgan and Horace would ruin you if they had a chance."

"How do you know this?"

"They were all against Jim. They fought him from every angle. He told me about it. Drinking was his outlet. It eventually caused his death."

"It's hard to think of a man having your love and then committing suicide."

She drew away from him. "Jim Dunphy was weak but he wasn't the type to commit suicide, Dan."

"What do you mean?"

She shrugged. "I just never believed he would do it. I still don't."

He eyed her closely. "Just what do you mean, Harriet? I want to know. There are a lot of things I don't know about Fort Costain."

"I'll tell you then. Cornish worked on Jim. Melva worked on him. There were times when Jim was too drunk to attend to his duties and the other officers had things their own way."

"Morgan and Horace?"

"Yes. And Kroft. Kroft hated field duty. Horace protected him. Morgan wanted Jim's command. Oh, it was terrible. I don't want to see it happen to you."

He drew her to him. "It won't."

"Cornish told my father about you. How you were sent out here to salvage your career." She looked up at him. "It was liquor, wasn't it, Dan?"

He flushed. "In a way."

"I remember the night we were at Tres Cabezas. Your screaming woke me up. I couldn't believe it was you. It was terrible."

He dropped his hands. "A man hates to see his inner soul stripped for inspection," he said quietly. "Perhaps we'd better forget about the two of us, Harriet."

She shook her head. "I can help you. My father had those nightmares after the war. His arm would bother him and he took to heavy drinking. It caused his separation from my mother. He fought it off out here." She looked up at him. "You will let me help you, Dan?"

"Yes," he promised. He kissed her. "We'll work it out together." He walked to the door and looked back at her. "You seem doomed to help men like me, Harriet."

She shook her head. "Not *doomed*, Dan. *Blessed.*"

Dan mounted Hardtack and turned him toward the road. He looked up at the mesa and at the smoke wreathing up from the unseen fort. Suddenly he smashed a fist down on his pommel. They might get him in the end but they'd have one hell of a battle before they did. A battle they'd never forget.

15

GILA BARNES was waiting in Dan's quarters with another man when Dan returned to the post. Gila jerked a thumb at his weather-beaten companion. "Sage Winters," he said. "Lives near Union. Come here to tell you something of interest."

Dan gripped the old man's hand. "Drink?" he asked.

Sage wet his lips. "Don't mind if I do."

Dan poured two drinks and handed them to his two guests. "What do you have to tell me, Sage?" he asked.

Sage drank half his liquor and wiped his mouth. "Like Gila says, I live near Union. I do some prospectin' in the hills when I want to get away from my old lady. I was up in the hills the last month or so. Didn't know the 'Paches was on the loose from San Ignacio. Anyways I never take chances with the bushy-headed bastards. I seen Old Cut

Lip's band in the hills near Skull Butte. Hair Rope, the misbegotten bastard, with with 'em. They headed into the malpais country."

Dan refilled the old man's glass.

Sage nodded and raised his glass in salute. "Coupla weeks later I'm far north in the malpais. Suddenly the goddamned country is thick with 'Paches. Tontos. Coyoteros. Even some of the Girls!"

"Girls?" asked Dan.

"He means Aravaipas," said Gila.

"Yeh," said Sage, "Parties of half a dozen or so, all riding into the Skull Butte country. I skites outa there and finds myself trapped in a damned box canyon. I'm back-trailing when I sees a mess of 'Paches camped in the canyon where the box canyon ends. Christ! It was enough to give a man the chills! I had to kill Bessie to keep her mouth shut."

"Bessie?" asked Dan.

Sage nodded soberly. "My old mule. She was a good one but had too big a mouth. I hides out on the canyon wall with a little water and grub, hoping the red bastards would pull out. They don't. They have a big feast. It was a dandy, Gila. They cooked an unborn foal in its mother's juices. Golden brown it was."

"Delicious," said Gila.

Sage grunted. "Gila is half heathen, Major Fayes."

"I've always thought so."

"Go to hell," said Gila with a sly grin.

Sage glanced wistfully at his glass. Dan filled it up. Sage brightened. "Waal, they had quite a *baile*. Plenty likker and food. Scalp dance. Hell, it was enough to make your hair stand on end. Screaming. Whooping. Hollering. There musta been at least a hundred and fifty bucks down there, with enough Henry rifles to equip a squadron. Brand-new they was! That old devil Black Wind squats in the middle of the uproar passin' out cartridges. He had boxes and boxes of 'em. The warriors whoop and holler, wavin' them damned rifles. Then they tortures a white man. By God, I got sick. Lost what little food I et. The poor bastard stays alive for hours, though you couldn't tell he was a man when they was done. I was tempted to blast him between the eyes with my big Sharps but I knowed they'd get me less'n I kilt myself."

Recall blew across the post. Horses trotted past the quarters. Sage swilled his liquor in his glass. "Can I have a cigar, Major?" he asked.

Dan gave him one and lit it. Sage puffed steadily. "Then old Black Wind makes a speech. It was a dandy. He tells them they got the White-eyes scairt to death. He says they cut 'em up at Sand Springs. That they raided Fort Costain and burned the stables. He goes on and on talkin' about what they done. How he can get all the rifles he wants from White-eyed friends for *pesh-klitso*."

"He means gold," said Gila.

Dan felt cold all over. He poured a drink. "Go on," he said quietly.

Sage sucked at his cigar. "He says the Long Knives are ascairt to come in after old Black Wind, the greatest of all chiefs. Funny thing though, he talks like *he* led the raids. Blind and old as he is."

Dan nodded. "We've suspected it."

"Waal, you can *bet* on it. That greasy old

mummy knows this country bettern' God who made it."

"You're sure you understood what he was saying?" asked Dan.

Gila grinned. "Sage talks 'Pache like a real quill. Seems as though Sage had a 'Pache squaw onct."

Sage licked his thin lips. "Yeh. Plump as a grouse. Soft as down. Kept her mouth shut when a man wanted to think."

Dan paced back and forth. "Seems like we're sitting on top of a powder magazine with the fuse lit."

He handed the old man a box of cigars and a bottle of mezcal. "Thanks, Sage."

Sage waved a dirty claw. "Fergit it. Glad to be of help."

"Did they mention who was running the guns in?"

"I caught somethin' about Ben Ducey. Didn't believe it. I've known Ben for years. We was livin' with sisters before the war. Apaches they was." The old man stood up and walked to the door. "Got to get back to my old woman," he said. *"Adios, amigos."* Suddenly he turned. "Gila, you keep that double-hinged jaw of yours shut about that squaw if you see my old lady. Hear?"

Gila nodded. Sage left. Gila looked at Dan. "I thought you might be interested in what Sage had to say."

"I was. The prospect scares me."

Gila nodded. "Yeh. But if we don't root Black Wind out it'll be a hell of a lot worse, Danny."

"One hundred and fifty blood-hungry bucks led by one of the greatest war chiefs of them all. It isn't a pleasant prospect, Gila."

"For this you're a soldier, Dan."

Dan nodded. "Yes."

Gila jerked a thumb at Dan's desk. "Sam Booth cleaned up Dunphy's room. He burned the trash. He said he thought you might want to look over that stuff." Gila left the quarters.

Dan poured a drink and lit a cigar. He looked at the things on his desk. An old leather corps badge from the cavalry outfit Dunphy had probably served with. A hunting case watch. A japanned pen case with several pens and steel points. A traveler's ink vial a quarter full of dried ink. Several tarnished sets of major's leaves. A dusty black velvet cap patch with the crossed sabers of the cavalry embroidered on it. Spare coat and overcoat buttons. An officer's belt plate.

Dan downed his drink. He wondered if Harriet would want these pitiful relics of the weak man she had thought she loved. He shrugged, opened a drawer and swept them into it. He shut it and then saw the folded papers lying on top of some of his own. They had been stained by water. He unfolded the top one. It consisted of notations on grading and re-enforcing the end of the paradeground to prevent further erosion. The second sheet was a list of post officers and their duties. The third was a note from Jim Moore containing a list of enlisted men who owed him money for drinks.

Dan lit his candle lantern and opened the last paper. It was a double list of figures. Each line of figures was dated. The left-hand column consisted of figures labeled "Pay." The right-hand column was of a greater sum with notations to the right of them. The notations were about liquor, furniture, silverware and other household and personal items. There were four dates, all of them the end of the mouth. The paper was hardly legible because of water stains.

Dan studied the faded writing. Possibly Dunphy's pay and his expenses. Yet a major's pay was more than the pay figures listed. They were a captain's pay. He walked outside. A trooper was passing. "Get Private Booth," said Dan. "Tell him to report to me here at once."

Dan was looking over the sheet again when he heard a tap on the door. The door opened and Trooper Sam Booth came in. "You wanted to see me, sir?"

Dan nodded. "Where did you find the things you left on my desk?"

"The stuff from Major Dunphy's room?"

"Yes."

"There was a niche in the closet. That stuff was in a cardboard box. Looked like water leaked through the roof. I guess it was overlooked when Major Dunphy's things was sent away to his folks at home."

Dan rubbed his jaw. Booth looked at the bottle. "Have a drink," said Dan.

"Yes, sir!"

Booth filled a glass and downed it. He looked at the paper on Dan's desk. "I can tell you about that, sir."

Dan looked up. "So?"

Booth nodded. "I was Major Dunphy's orderly too. Got kicked out of the job when Captain Morgan took over. Major Dunphy was a real officer. Like you, sir. Always had a drink or a smoke for an enlisted man."

"Keep talking."

"I was cleaning out the washhouse one afternoon. I sneaked in here to see if Major Dunphy might have a dollop left in one of his bottles. I was coming up the hallway when I hears him arguing with somebody."

"So, being a good soldier, you went right out to the washhouse again."

Booth looked pained. "I stuck around figuring he might need me."

"Listening."

"Well . . . yes, sir. Anyways it was something about money. Seems as though this other officer was spending a hell of a lot more than he was drawing."

"No crime in that."

"I guess not. Well, the argument got hot. Dunphy says something about the Inspector General. Captain Cornish don't seem worried."

Dan looked up quickly. "Captain Cornish?"

"Yes, sir. I always wondered where he got his money. The whole damned post knows he ain't got a cent beyond what he draws as surgeon."

"How long ago was the argument?"

"About three days before Major Dunphy shot himself."

"I see." Dan fingered the paper on his desk.

"I remember that paper because I put it away in with his other papers. One day he comes in and asks me where I put it. I told him and he took it out. Today was the first time I saw it since then."

Dan stood up. "All right, Booth. One thing. Keep your mouth shut about this."

The trooper saluted and left.

Dan sat staring at the papers on his desk. Dunphy had had trouble with Cornish. Something about Cornish's high expenses. Then Dunphy had committed suicide. Yet Harriet had said Jim Dunphy wouldn't have done it. Then Dan remembered the night someone had lain in wait for him in his quarters and had shot at him. Cold sweat worked down his sides, soaking his shirt.

Dan lit a cigar and dropped on his coat. Kroft had had gold dust. Kroft had shot and killed Ben Ducey out in the hills. An attempted escape. More likely the *ley del fuego*. Let the prisoner run and *then* execute him.

Dan put on his cap and crossed to headquarters. "Linke," he said to the little orderly clerk, "go and get Mister Kroft."

"He's under arrest in quarters, sir."

"Dammit! Go get him!"

Linke scurried from the room. He was back in five minutes. "He isn't there, sir."

"Did you look for him?"

"Yes, sir."

"Get the officer of the guard."

Linke brought back Halloran of C Company. He wore his sash across his chest signifying his duty as officer of the guard. "Halloran, find Mister Kroft. Bring him here under arrest."

Halloran looked strangely at Dan, saluted and left.

Dan waited impatiently. He'd wring the truth out of that goddamned shavetail if he had to beat him to a pulp.

The sun was long gone when Halloran returned. "We found him, sir," he said quietly, "out at the range. I left a man to watch him."

"Dammit! I told you to bring him here!"

"Yes, sir. But I had to leave him where he was. You see, sir . . . he's dead."

Dan hit the floor. "The hell you say? Apaches?"

Halloran shook his head. "His service pistol is in his hand. He shot himself, sir."

"Come on!" Dan ran across the parade-ground and down the wooden stairs that led to the bottoms. He ran through the darkness to the firing butts.

"He's over there, sir," called Halloran.

"In the trees beside the creek."

Dan pushed his way through the brush. A corporal leaned on his carbine beside the sprawled body. Kroft lay on his back with his eyes open. A bluish hole showed at his left temple. A little blood and matter had oozed from the purplish hole.

Dan knelt beside the body. He touched it. It was still a little warm. Dan stood up. He looked at Halloran. "Get a detail to take the body up to the post."

"I wonder why he did it?" asked Halloran.

Dan shrugged and walked off through the darkness. His foot struck something. He bent to pick it up. It was a short-handled spade. He eyed it and then looked back at Kroft. He placed the spade against a tree and walked up to the post. Dunphy a suicide. Ben Ducey shot down by Kroft. Kroft dead by his own hand. Dan suddenly felt as though he were in the coils of some twisted problem, impossible to decipher. The smiling smooth face of Myron Cornish seemed to show up in the shadows.

16

FORREST KROFT was laid out in the hospital covered by a sheet. The thin material outlined his face. A strong draft blew in from the open door and swayed the lamps on their chains. The shadows covered the still form or swept away from it as the lamps moved. Dan stood beside the body and drew the sheet back from the bluish face. The lips had drawn back slightly from the white teeth.

Feet grated on the gritty floor. Dan turned. Sergeant French approached him. "Seems like the ones you least expect to kill themselves are the ones that do it. Now I never thought of a man like Mister Kroft going this way."

Dan lit a cigar and studied the handsome face, now cold in death. "Kroft was right-handed, French."

"Yes."

Dan pointed at the hole in the temple. "Then how could he have shot himself in the left temple. It's possible, but damned awkward."

"By God, sir! I never thought of that. What does it mean?"

"I'm not sure. Was the slug extracted?"

"Yes, sir. Forty-five caliber. One cartridge had been fired in his Colt."

Dan drew the sheet over Kroft's face. "You were here when Major Dunphy committed suicide?"

"Yes."

"That was also a forty-five?"

French rubbed his jaw. "I'm not sure."

"What do you mean?"

"His Colt had been fired once. Captain Cornish extracted the slug."

"So?"

"I'm not sure it was .45 caliber, sir. It seemed smaller to me. More like a .41, but I was never sure. I had forgotten about it until tonight."

"But you aren't sure?"

"No, sir."

Dan relit his cigar, eying the noncom

over the flare of the match. "Keep your mouth shut about this, French."

"I will, sir. What is it . . . murder?"

Dan threw down the match. "I don't know. Good night, French."

Dan went to headquarters. Woodridge was still at work. He looked up as Dan entered. "I have the roster of your scouts, sir," he said.

Dan held out his hand. He scanned the list. His junior officers were Halloran and Sykes, both men of promise. Sergeant Major Haley. Medical Sergeant French. Sergeants Bostwick and Cutter. Corporals Denton, Ferris, Moylan and Crispin. He scanned the list of troopers. "We've made quite a drain on B Company, Woodridge," he said.

Woodridge nodded. "B has always been the best company in the squadron, sir." He grinned. "Captain Horace has been raising hell about losing his men. He and Captain Morgan have been sympathizing with each other." Woodridge leaned back in his chair. "Can I speak plainly, sir?"

"Certainly."

"You've done a good job so far, sir. In *some* ways. You have been rather ruthless in not sparing the feelings of Morgan and Horace. I don't think they'll take much more of it."

Dan waved a hand. "Have you started to prepare a report on Kroft's death?"

"Not yet, sir."

"Hold off on it for awhile."

"It isn't regulation, sir."

Dan looked steadily at the adjutant. "It isn't regulation if the report you submit is erroneous, is it?"

Woodridge stared at Dan. "No, sir."

Dan turned to the door. "I may have more information for you before long on the subject."

Dan tapped on the door of the surgeon's quarters. Melva opened it. She smiled as she saw Dan. "I haven't seen much of you, Dan."

"I've been busy, Melva."

"Do come in."

He followed her through the hallway to the snug living room. A fire burned in the fireplace. It was then that Dan realized

Melva was not wearing a dress. Only a thin wrapper clung to her full figure. As she walked ahead of him he could see the full length of her legs silhouetted against the firelight. She turned. "You must excuse me," she said. "I thought it was Myron when you knocked. I was getting ready to dress."

"I'm sorry I interrupted you. I wanted to see your brother."

"He's at Captain Morgan's quarters. He should be back shortly."

She made no move to leave the room. "Would you like a drink, Dan?"

He nodded. She filled the glass and brought it to him, looking up into his face. The fragrance of her perfume and body drifted about him. She was expecting something. Dan took the glass and turned away.

Melva sat down in the big armchair and looked curiously at him. "What's wrong, Dan?"

"Nothing."

"I don't believe you. You're under a strain."

"Yes," he admitted.

"Because of Forrest Kroft?"

He looked at her. "Partly. I just added to the trouble."

"Myron said he always suspected Forrest would crack someday."

Dan sipped his wine. "Sometimes I think your brother is more interested in the mind than he is in the body."

"I agree. He seemed to know Jim Dunphy would kill himself."

"A prophet."

She looked at him queerly. "Why do you want to talk with Myron tonight?" she asked.

"We had a little trouble about some requisitions of his."

She paled a little and touched her smooth throat with a slim hand. "Myron gets angry when line officers question him about his duties."

"He's a soldier, no matter what his duty is. As his commanding officer it is *my* duty to question him."

She leaned her head back against the chair. "I see. He has been talking about leaving the service."

"To go into private practice?"

"I don't think so. He wants to make a great deal of money."

Dan looked about the expensively furnished room. "It seems as though he has already done well for himself."

She lowered her lids and studied him. Then she stood up and got the decanter. "Let me fill your glass, Dan."

As she came close to him her leg pressed against his. He stood up and drew her close. She did not resist. Her body was soft and warm, hardly protected by the thin material of the wrapper. She placed the decanter on the table and slid her smooth arms about his neck, drawing his face down to hers. Her lips parted as she kissed him.

Minutes drifted past as they stood there. There was a roaring in Dan's ears. She was no amateur at lovemaking and once again he thought of Kitty St. Clair in Washington. She turned away from him and walked to the couch, looking back over her shoulder. Dan followed her and placed his hands on her full hips. She turned and sat down, drawing him down to her. "You're tired," she whispered.

The fire was burning low. There was no other light in the big room. Her breath came quickly as he kissed her and passed his hands over her full body. "Come back later," she said softly. "Myron is going off the post tonight."

"I must see him."

"Not tonight. You're angry. It will only end in a quarrel."

He straightened up and looked at her. "What makes you say that?"

She kissed him. "I know. Please go now, Dan."

He stood up and looked down at her. She was like a lazy cat crouching there, soft and warm.

"Come back about nine," she said.

Dan picked up his forage cap and left. It wasn't until he was in his own quarters that he realized she had staved off the meeting between him and her brother.

Dan peeled off his shell jacket and scaled his hat at a chair. He dropped on his bunk and reached for the bottle of mezcal in the cabinet. He drank deeply, again and again, thinking fleetingly of Harriet Moore but more often of Melva Cornish.

Tattoo rang out across the post. Dan opened his eyes. The room was dark, the candle lantern having guttered out. The darkness seemed to swim around him and Dan knew he was as close to being drunk as he could be. He dropped his legs to the floor and ran his tongue over his dry lips. He reached for the half-empty bottle and then shook his head. He picked up a towel, thrust his Colt beneath his waistband and headed for the washhouse. He soused his face in the water and slowly dried himself. It was close to ten o'clock.

He went back to his room, lit the lantern and dressed quickly. His head still swam a little as he blew out the lantern and walked outside. The post area was dark. He crossed quickly toward the surgeon's quarters. A horse whinnied from the darkness. Cornish's fine mare was tethered at the back of the quarters. Cantle and pommel packs were on the mare and the saddlebags bulged. The rear door was part way open. Dan could hear voices inside.

"You've got money, Melva," said Cornish. "They won't bother you."

"But why are you leaving, Myron? What has happened?"

Dan looked through the doorway. Cornish had his back to Dan. He was dressed in field uniform, booted and spurred.

Cornish waved a hand. "I haven't time to tell you about it now. Fayes suspects something. I can't take a chance on him having me arrested for investigation."

Melva stared at him. "What have you done?"

"I told you I don't have time. His orderly told me he's asleep. When he wakes up he'll be here, if you've played your cards right."

"I did. I'm sick of this business, Myron! First it was Jim Dunphy. Then Ellis Morgan. Now Dan Fayes. What am I to you? A lure to keep your superiors from watching you too closely?"

Cornish slipped a Colt into his holster.

"All you need to know is that you've done a damned good job."

"I hate it!"

"Yes. But you like the money that goes with it. It's all over now."

"He'll suspect something. How long can I hold him?"

Cornish laughed. "You'll hold him all right. I can trust you for that."

She turned her face away from him. "There's something you've been hiding from me. I worked with you believing you'd make enough money and stop your illicit dealings. Why can't you stop now? Dan doesn't know enough to arrest you."

Cornish picked his hat from the table. "Listen," he said quietly. "Fayes was questioning Sergeant French. He suspects something about Kroft's death."

Her eyes widened. "What? It was suicide, wasn't it?"

"No! Kroft killed Ben Ducey to make him keep his mouth shut. Fayes would have wormed the truth out of him. I couldn't take a chance on that!"

"What are you driving at, Myron?"

"Kroft knew I had a cache down near the creek. He went down there to find it when I wouldn't give him any more dust. I followed him. We had words. I killed him."

Her hand went to her throat. "Why didn't you tell me? They'll think *I* had something to do with it."

"Dammit! I told you they had nothing on you. Keep Fayes here tonight. I've got to have time to get away!"

Dan eased through the doorway. Melva's eyes widened in terror. Cornish whirled. He jerked his Colt free and swept the Argand lamp from the table, crashing it to the floor. Melva screamed as Dan closed in. Cornish lashed at Dan with his Colt. Dan blocked the blow and hit the surgeon in the belly. Cornish grunted and dropped the pistol. His strong hands closed about Dan's throat. They went back against the wall. Cornish tightened his grip. Dan brought up a knee into the surgeon's groin.

Cornish grunted. He kicked Dan in the belly. He snatched up a glass pitcher and struck hard at Dan. The pitcher shattered on Dan's head. He went down on his knees with the shock. Blood veiled his face. Cornish laughed wildly as he battered at Dan's head with the remains of the pitcher. Dan gripped Cornish by the knees and dumped him back over the table. He hammered blindly at the smooth face, feeling his knuckles rip against the teeth.

Melva slammed the door shut. Cornish rolled sideways as Dan felt his fists smash teeth. The surgeon wrapped his long legs about Dan's waist and raised his upper body. Dan fell backward with Cornish on top of him. Cornish broke free and scrabbled for his pistol in the darkness. He gripped it and swung hard. The barrel clipped Dan across the side of the head. Dan fell behind the table.

"Don't shoot!" screamed Melva. "You'll rouse the post!"

Dan came up from behind the table to meet a savage slashing blow of the pistol. He hit the floor hard, dimly hearing the smash of boots against the floor. The door opened and slammed and then Dan went down into a pit of swirling darkness.

Dimly he heard the grating of feet on the floor and the low talking. He opened his eyes. Ellis Morgan was standing with his arm about Melva Cornish's shoulders. Captain Andrew Horace leaned against the wall looking down at Dan.

Dan touched his slashed skull. It throbbed like a drum. There was a lump over his left ear.

"Get up," said Morgan thinly, "you drunken scum!"

The strong odor of whisky clung about Dan. An empty bottle lay at his side. He got to his feet and stood there swaying, holding his battered head. Then he looked at Melva. "Where is he?"

She drew her ripped dress closer together. "Who?"

"Your brother."

"It's a good thing he isn't here," said Horace. "He'd have killed you for what you tried to do."

Melva turned her face away. "It was terrible. He knew Myron was gone. I was just getting ready for bed. He tried to attack me. I struck him with the pitcher. Thank

God he went down."

A cold feeling came over Dan. "She's lying," he said.

Morgan walked toward Dan. "Are you armed?" he asked.

Dan shook his head.

Morgan drew his Colt. "I'm placing you under arrest, Major Fayes," he said.

"On what charge?"

"Drunkenness. Attempted rape. You'd better come with me."

Dan looked at Melva. "Tell him the truth!"

She looked away.

Dan gripped Horace by the arm. "Cornish was here. He admitted he murdered Kroft. We fought. He's riding away from here right now while we stand here like idiots!"

Horace drew away from Dan. "You've ruined yourself," he said. "I knew it was only a matter of time. Riding the officers and destroying the squadron with your insane ideas. Proving what Captain Cornish said about you."

"What was that?" asked Dan quietly.

Horace smirked. "He prepared a report saying you were an alcoholic and unfit for command. He gave it to Captain Morgan and myself. We're forwarding it to Department Headquarters. You're through, Fayes. And I'm damned glad of it."

Morgan jerked his head. "Come on," he said.

Dan walked to the door. Unless Cornish was caught there was no way he could clear himself. He wiped the blood from his face. A dry wind swept about him as he rounded the corner of the building. The gully was just to his left. He lurched against Morgan, and the heavy man stumbled. Dan ducked and darted to one side. He plunged down the eroded slope as Morgan cursed. The Colt flamed in the darkness. Dan hit the ground hard and raced through the darkness toward the creek.

Horace and Morgan were yelling for the guard. Dan reached the trees. He ran to the creek bank and jumped into the shallow waters. He splashed across and gained the far shore. The yelling grew fainter behind him as he trotted through the trees toward the north. The fat was in the fire now, but he had to get Myron Cornish. He needed a horse and a gun. Moore's Ranch was his best bet. He looked back over his shoulder. A lantern bobbed about on the edge of the paradeground. He increased his pace although his battered head pounded fiercely.

There was a faint moon rising in the eastern sky. The wind swept across the hills, moaning softly. Dan crossed the creek again and worked his way up a slope. Two miles further on he saw the dim outline of Moore's Ranch. Only one light showed in the big house.

Dan stopped and listened. There were no sounds of pursuit. He stood there with the faint moonlight shining on his bloody face, and there was cold hate in his eyes. Then he pushed his way through the brush toward the ranch.

17

THE wind soughed about the ranch buildings and flapped the wagon covers. The bunkhouse was off to one side, dark and silent. Dan padded across the yard behind the main building, where one window showed yellow light. The house seemed closed for the night. The heavy shutters were closed. He tried the front door. It was bolted.

Dan walked around and tried the back door. It swung open easily at his touch. He eased himself inside the dark kitchen. The building was as quiet as the grave except for the steady ticking of the waggle-tailed clock on the kitchen wall. Dan crossed the dark barroom to the large room which served as the general store. He lit a match and looked about the well-stocked chamber. Light showed in a thin line beneath a door at the rear.

He eased the doorknob and opened the

door a crack. It was a bedroom. Harriet's. The bed was still made. The lamp flared a little in the draft. The room was empty of life. A closet door gaped open. Some clothing lay on the floor. Dan shoved back his cap and looked about with a puzzled expression on his battered face.

An icy feeling formed within him. Harriet was gone, and he suddenly knew she had not left of her own free will. He put out the lamp and returned to the store. He helped himself to a Colt .45 and cartridges. A Henry rifle. Canteens, food and blankets. He buckled a gunbelt about his waist and slid the Colt into it. The rest of the things he placed in a sack. He blew out the lamp and walked out of the building.

In the big stable he picked a stocky dun and saddled it. He formed cantle and pommel packs and lashed them in place. Then he led the dun out into the wide yard. On a sudden thought he walked to the bunkhouse and tried the door. It opened. He lit a match. A man lay face downward on the packed-earth floor. The back of his gray head was stained with blood. It was Sim

Eames, one of the employees.

Dan rolled the little man over. He was still alive. Dan wiped the face with cold water. Eames opened his eyes. "Jesus," he said, "my head's explodin'."

"You'll live. What happened?"

Eames sat up and gingerly touched the back of his head. "I helped Miss Harriet close up for the night. Then I comes over here. Joe Steiner and Casey Duncan had gone into Mesquite Wells. Whilst I was thinking of goin' to bed I hears this horse outside. I goes to the door and sees Captain Cornish out there. He asks me if he can get some supplies. He says he's leavin' Fort Costain. I tells him Miss Harriet has closed for the night. When I turns away from him it seems like the floor comes up to hit me in the face. That's all I know."

Dan stood up. "Harriet's gone," he said. "Cornish has taken her with him."

"She wouldn't go anywheres with that cold-eyed bastard."

"She probably had nothing to say about it. Listen, Sim, you didn't see me here."

"I get it."

"When the other men get back I want you to go up to the post and get hold of Gila Barnes. Tell *him*, and him only, that I've gone after Cornish."

"Keno!"

Dan left the bunkhouse and swung up on the dun. He spurred it toward the road. The wind shifted. He heard the thud of hoofs on the road in the direction of the fort. He looked back. A dark group of horsemen topped a rise. Troopers. He kneed the dun off the road into the brush and headed for the creek. Odds were that Cornish had gone north. If he had gone south toward Tres Cabezas he would run the risk of being picked up.

Dan crossed the creek and rode swiftly toward the north.

It was close to dawn when he noticed the bitter odor of wood smoke. A banner of gray smoke hung low along the creek bottoms. He drew rein on a rise and looked down toward a burned-out ranchhouse. The wind fanned the huge beds of ashes, revealing bright eyes of fires. He rode slowly toward it. In the graying light he saw a dog sprawled across a flat rock. His skull had been cleft by a terrific blow.

Dan slid from his saddle, slipping his Henry rifle from its sheath. The wind moaned through the trees, fanning the beds of ashes into fiery life. Scattered about the trampled ground were battered pieces of furniture. Two men lay beneath the trees, with the curious lopsided look a smashed skull gives the faces of the dead. Dan picked up a war club. The tip was clotted with blood and hair.

Dan wet his lips. The air was oppressive with the heat from the embers. Unshod pony tracks pocked the earth, with a great litter of empty cartridge cases scattered about them.

The Apaches were getting bolder. The small ranch was no more than three miles from Mesquite Wells. Then the ghastly thought struck him that Cornish might have run into them.

Dan walked about the area in the graying light. The pony tracks led north through a draw. He followed them and then stopped. Mingled with the unshod tracks were those of two shod horses, a big one and a smaller one. Dan squatted by the trail looking north toward the hills. A worm of bitter thought crept slowly into his mind. Cornish was the mastermind behind the gun-running. The Apaches had allowed Ben Ducey free passage through their land. *Why not Cornish?*

Dan lit a cigar and passed a dirty hand across his sore jaw. Where else could Cornish go? Harriet wouldn't have gone with him without resistance. In Mesquite Wells, Union or Beasley someone would have noticed she was a prisoner. The pieces of thought moved about, adjusted themselves and then formed an unholy pattern. He was sure Cornish was with the only friends he had . . . the Apaches he had so well supplied with rifles.

Dan went back to the dun. He mounted it and passed from the ruined ranch, never looking back.

The trail was well marked, revealing the contempt the raiders felt toward any pursuers. Here a pair of gaudy galluses hung over a mesquite bush. There a battered clock lay in the dust.

By noon Dan was high above the valley of the San Ignacio, looking northeast to where a plume of smoke drifted upward. Burning ranch or Apache signal fire?

Dan kneed the dun to one side, following a faintly defined trail. He couldn't go back. Morgan might have a patrol looking for him. Going ahead didn't make much sense. What could he do against a war party of blood-hungry Apaches? He wasn't even sure Harriet was with them.

The lone man to the rear led his horse across the flats, kneeling now and then to examine the ground. Then he would look up at the ragged hills and plod on.

Dan touched his cracked lips with the tip of his tongue. He had had no water since the day before. The sun beat down on the hollow, making the rocks almost too hot to touch. Dan slid his Henry rifle forward and sighted the lone man. The sights seemed to swim in the hazy heat. The dun nickered from the bottom of the hollow.

Dan studied the approaching man and then stood up. There was no mistaking the battered Kossuth hat and the ewe-necked roan. Gila looked up and jumped to one side, raising his long-barreled Spencer. Then he stared and ran to the roan. He mounted and spurred it up the slope. He slid from the saddle and eyed Dan. "Jesus," he said, "you leave a trail like a travois."

Dan grinned. "I thought I was pretty careful."

Gila spat. "It's a damned good thing I found yuh before yuh got any farther into these goddamned hills."

"How's the water?"

"Just enough for a swallow or two." Gila unhooked a huge canteen and handed it to Dan. Dan sipped a little and then wet his scarf. He wiped the dun's mouth with it.

Gila squatted on the hot rocks, oblivious to the heat, and studied Dan through half-closed eyes. "There was hell to pay when you escaped. Morgan took command and ordered Charlie Norman to go after you. Norman refused. Morgan put him under arrest. Then we get a message that Black Wind struck the mines at Union. Killed seven miners and set fire to one of the buildings. Got away with thirty horses and mules. Morgan gets scared. He orders out the scouts."

"So?"

Gila waved a dusty arm. "They're back there five miles. Denny Halloran is leadin' 'em. Morgan ordered me to track you down. I leaves the post and waits for Halloran. I didn't want to see him get into this country and get cut up."

"Will Halloran attempt to arrest me?"

Gila shook his head. "Morgan had enough sense to keep his mouth shut about that hassle in Cornish's quarters. Ain't no one knows about it but Morgan, Horace and Norman, exceptin' me of course, and I won't talk."

"So?"

"This is your chance. The chance you was so all-fired eager to get. Yuh got your scouts. Yuh got me. All we have to do is surround one hundred and fifty 'Paches in their own country and make 'em say Mama."

"They're up there ahead of me. In the

hills. And I think Cornish is with them."
Dan puffed at his cigar. "Let's get the scouts."

Gila walked to his roan and drew Dan's new Winchester from its slings. "I thought yuh might want this. Brought along some mocs for yuh too."

"Thoughtful of you, son."

Gila shrugged. "By the way," he said with a sly grin, "how was it?"

Dan looked up. "What?"

"Melva Cornish, yuh idjit."

Dan spat. "I didn't get that far. It was a rigged job, Gila. Melva was just giving Cornish time to make his break."

Gila shook his head. "Just when yuh was makin' time too. Oh, well."

They mounted and rode down the slope with the late afternoon sun shining against their dusty faces.

It was dusk when Gila and Dan rode into the bivouac. Halloran had picked a good place for it, on a slope with a clear view of the surrounding terrain. The horses and four pack mules were in a hollow on individual picket lines. The cooking fires were already out.

Halloran showed a look of relief on his lean face when he saw Dan. "I wasn't too keen on this jaunt, sir."

Dan looked quickly at him. "Why?"

"The scouts were the major's idea. The men seemed to think you'd lead them. It makes a difference when someone else takes over the command."

Dan nodded.

Halloran swept an arm to indicate the command. "Each scout carries one hundred rounds of Henry rifle ammunition. Twenty-five for the Colts. In reserve we have another two hundred for each carbine and twenty-five more for each Colt. Water for one more day. Cooking rations for two more days and enough embalmed beef to carry us along for three more days."

"You brought the rawhide boots for the horses and mules?"

"Yes, sir. Two sets for each animal. The men are wearing one pair with an extra pair tied to their saddles."

"There is water for the animals in a *tinaja*

behind those rocks. A little green but palatable."

A trooper took the two tired horses to water them. Dan squatted beside a rock and accepted a cigar from Halloran. "Get Sid Sykes," he said.

The junior officer came through the darkness and squatted beside Denny Halloran. Sergeant Major Haley loomed behind him. He grinned as he saw Dan.

Dan lit his cigar. "The Apaches struck near Mesquite Wells, evidently after hitting Union. I trailed them into some malpais and lost them. But they're up ahead of us somewhere."

He took his cigar from his mouth. "We'll stay here until midnight and then move out. Gila, you take a corporal and four men and leave an hour ahead of us. Keep us posted by courier. We'll cross the flats and take that shallow canyon northeast of here. If we don't run into them we'll bivouac near the place we found Ben Ducey."

"Keno," said Gila.

Dan turned to Halloran. "I want a quiet march. Send Mister Sykes to check each man before we leave. I want no jingling, squeaking or knocking. We'll travel like ghosts."

"Yes, sir."

Dan yawned. "I want some sleep. Keep a moving guard below these rocks. If anything looks suspicious wake me up!"

Dan made his bed beneath an overhang. He lay there a long time listening to the muted voices of the men. More than one of them had eyed his battered face but had said nothing. There was a feeling of hopelessness in him. He doubted if Cornish had any interest in Harriet beyond using her as a hostage. It wouldn't be past the surgeon to leave her with the Apaches when he pulled foot. The rest of it wasn't fit to think about.

The command moved out at an easy walk. The saddles were cold and there had been no coffee. The men were sour. The moon shed enough light for them to see their way. It was as though they were moving on another planet or as the last survivors of humanity on a deserted earth.

The first courier met them a mile from the canyon mouth. Gila was far up the canyon. No signs of life. But they had found tracks. Mingled with the tracks of the Apache horses were those of two shod horses. A big stallion and a small mare.

The second courier met them at the designated bivouac area. Gila and Corporal Moylan had gone deeper into the hills and would return during the day. The command went into a fireless bivouac, eating stringy embalmed beef.

Dan allowed fires of dry wood just after dawn for heating coffee. The men slept heavily after their slim meal. Dan sat for a long time scanning the hazy hills with Halloran's field-glasses, but he might as well have saved his eyes. Not even a wisp of dust moved in those barren heights. Water was the big problem for Dan's command. The water at the bivouac served to refill the canteens and the horses and then was gone. The small water casks on the mules were kept filled as a reserve.

Corporal Moylan reported back at noon. "Gila has gone deeper into the hills," he said. "He doesn't like the looks of the canyon up ahead. The walls are sheer. A perfect place for an ambush. However, sir, there is a sort of rough pass which cuts to the west. Beyond that pass is a way to circle far behind the area where Gila thinks the Apaches have holed up."

"So?"

Moylan shrugged. "Gila is not sure of how we can get into the Apaches' canyon. It's a long shot, sir."

Dan eyed the rough map Moylan had sketched in the sand. "What about water?"

"He says there is water at Roca Roja. Big natural tanks there. They run dry about this time."

Dan nodded. "Halloran," he said quietly, "we'll pull out at dusk. Moylan will guide us."

The book has explicit rules on the march of cavalry. Space out to fifty-five paces, stagger the files to keep the dust down and give the mounts a chance to breathe. Unbit to graze, even on the shortest halts. Halt ten minutes on the hour and allow forty minutes every sixth hour for watering. Trot twenty minutes every second hour and lead for the full hour preceding water call. Treat a horse like the best friend you've got, and talk to him like a brother.

But how can a command be spread out to fifty-five paces and staggered twenty yards to the right when you're traveling in a narrow slot of a canyon no more than fifty feet wide at the bottom? Forty minutes every sixth hour is fine for watering when you have an unlimited supply of water and you have six hours to travel in. You can't trot big cavalry mounts in rocky country when a hoof striking a stone can be heard by Apache ears for an eighth of a mile.

Dan tugged at his dun's reins. "Come on, *amigo*," he said to himself, "we've thrown away the book."

The day's heat hung in the narrow canyon like an issue blanket, forcing rivulets of sweat to break out on bodies and soak dusty uniforms. The command traveled silently in a heavy cloak of sweat-soaked wool, the acid smell of horses, the sweetish odor of damp leather. Even the moon did not penetrate the narrow slot. Thirty-seven men plunging through the darkness following an unknown trail to face four times their number of Apaches in the hostiles' back yard.

The pass was worse than the canyon. Great shattered heaps of rock obstructed the way, forcing the scouts to wind through a bewildering trail. Catclaw, cholla and prickly pear reached out thorny hands to tear at the soldiers dusty clothing. Here fragments of the moonlight speckled their dirty faces. Each man worried only about himself and his horse, now and then looking up to see the sweat-soaked man ahead of him, leading his dusty horse.

Dan looked back along the struggling column. Doubts gathered in his mind like buzzards settling on the dead. The one thing that kept him going was the fact that he had one sure weapon. The white man's ability to outthink the savage. Even of this he wasn't too sure, for old Black Wind had proved quite a few times that he could think himself.

The gray light of false dawn filtered down

on the little command. Dan turned to Denny Halloran. "Bivouac up that slope."

The area was a jumble of craggy rock, well armed with thorny vegetation. To the right rose a great knife-blade of a ridge, seemingly impossible to climb. Ahead of them was more of the country through which they had just traveled. Dan looked at his men, held in yellow-legged discipline. He beckoned to Haley. "Pass the word around that a white woman is in the hands of the Apaches."

Haley looked at Dan. "It will help, sir."

The whites of the men's eyes showed up against their tanned faces, coated with dust. They didn't say much, but there was a perceptible tightening in the command. Hands closed on pistol butts. They looked at each other and then went to take care of their horses. Tracking down hostile Apaches was one thing; saving a white woman from greasy exploring hands was another.

18

THE scouts were far below Dan as he stopped for a breather. Gila looked down from a rock slab. "Winded?" he asked with a sly grin.

Dan's breath was harsh in his throat. He looked up at the gaunt scout, perched like a crow on the lip of the rock. "Hell, yes," he gasped.

Gila cut a chew. "I got fifteen years on yuh, Dan."

"Yes, you bastard, but you're part mountain goat."

Gila chuckled as he slipped the chew into his mouth. "Never knew who my pa was, Dan."

"*I* know."

Dan leaned back against a rock. The heat seemed to shift about in heavy veils. They had been on the move all morning since Gila had found the Apaches. There were none on this side of the ridge according to the scout.

Dan slanted his hat brim over his reddened eyes and looked west. The terrain was fantastic. Frosty blues and cavalry-scarf yellows; broiled lobster-claw reds and hazy purples; grassy greens and dull golds. All of it blended together in a phantasmagoria of color.

"You're sure Harriet is still alive?" he asked quietly.

"Yeh. I think I seen her. Riding with the squaws. Cornish was with Black Wind."

Dan forced himself to his feet. His left moccasin had split along one side. His Winchester butt was scarred from his using it as an alpenstock to aid the hazardous ascent.

Gila went on tirelessly and then dropped to his knees. He waved a hand to Dan. Dan went to his knees and snaked along behind the scout, brushing against rock you could fry bacon on.

Gila was crouched in a cleft like a lizard. He shoved back his battered hat and wiped the collected sweat from his lined face. "Look," he said.

Below them a wide canyon cut like a

trough through the harsh earth. The far wall was hung with great masses of rock waiting for the next frost to loosen them enough for their downward plunge to the great talus slope far below. Here the canyon had a great indentation in it, caused by a naked shoulder of rock that thrust like a ship's prow into the trough. At the end of the shoulder was the mouth of another canyon, narrow and shadowy. A wisp of smoke drifted up from it. Along the base of the far wall was an indistinct line leading to a place where a humped ridge of rock followed the direction of the canyon wall.

Gila shifted his chew. "Yuh see that low ridge?"

"Yes."

"Behind that is a deep gully. Like a natural trench. That ridge is like a fort wall with loopholes in it."

"So?"

Gila eyed Dan. "This is the place. Holy ground it is for the Tontos. They've never been rooted outa here. In '63 the California Volunteer Cavalry tried to root 'em out. Lost twelve killed and seventeen wounded.

In '68 a squadron tried to get in here. They was badly cut up."

"I thought no troops had ever been in here."

"They ain't. The Californians got it ten miles from here in the canyon I come up. Full of twists and turns it is. A dozen warriors could hold it against a regiment. Believe me, Dan, there ain't been a yellow-leg in here yet."

"We're here."

Gils spat. "Yeh. Where? Behind this ridge. All Black Wind has to do is hole up behind that low ridge. Yuh can't get at 'em from the south. They got a fine field of fire there. Yuh can't get at 'em from the north. That rock shoulder cuts into the canyon. Look, the canyon ain't wide enough for a wagon to get through. Yuh figger on sliding down from here? In daylight you'd be cut to pieces. At night you'd lose half your men on the way and the rest would chew Apaches slugs once they hit the bottom. Now why in hell's name did yuh want to come in here?"

Dan uncased his glasses. Gila shaded them with his stinking Kossuth hat. Dan studied the far wall. Gila was right.

"They got a cinch here," said Gila, "Ain't no one gonna pry 'em out. The wimmen and kids is up that narrow canyon. It's a box with a damned dangerous trail outn it. Sage told me that. So the wimmen puts up the wickiups. They roast mezcal and broils horsemeat. They got water in there. Natural tanks, always in shade. Holds water most of the year. The bucks take it easy with a few warriors on guard."

Dan looked down toward the low ridge. There was a movement in the brush. A warrior walked past an open area. The sun glinted dully on the brass trim of his Henry rifle.

Dan put down the glasses. It was a tactical problem hard enough to analyze when a man was at his best. Lack of sleep and short rations hadn't helped Dan's weariness. He flogged his tired brain. *Always attempt to make the enemy think you are in force. Frighten them if possible. Trust in your luck.*

Using forty men to delude the Apaches into thinking he was in force would stretch things wire-thin. How in God's name could he frighten them? They were secure in their ancient natural fortress. Trusting in luck wasn't much of a sheet anchor to windward.

Dan looked north. "What's up there?"

"The bitchiest jumble of rocks yuh ever saw."

"Can we get up there from where we are?"

"Yeh. But what then?"

Dan rubbed his bristly jaw. The skin was taut from wind and sunburn. He remembered then he had cursed Trumpeter Criswell for letting the sun flash on his instrument just that very day. A trumpet had a brassy, far-carrying voice. He mentally placed that piece of the puzzle to one side for future use.

"Let's go," said Dan.

They worked their way down the steep side of the ridge. The men were scattered among the boulders, breathing hard in the heavy heat. Halloran, Sykes and Haley squatted in front of Dan. He wiped the sweat from his face and then sketched a map on the sand at his feet. "Mister Sykes will take a corporal and seven men back down this canyon to a point where they can climb the ridge and look down into the next canyon."

"I saw a place about a mile and half back," said Sykes.

"You will take Trumpeter Criswell as one of your men," Sykes looked puzzled.

"Halloran," continued Dan, "you will take the bulk of the scouts up to where Gila and I just were. Take all the ammunition you can carry. I want absolute silence in the climb and while you are up there."

Halloran nodded.

Dan looked at Sergeant Major Haley. "You will accompany me and Gila. I want eight men. The best shots and the toughest men in the unit."

Shadows were beginning to form in the canyon. The men eyed Dan. "At the first light of dawn, Mister Sykes, I want Criswell to lip onto that trumpet and put some spit into it!"

Sykes wet dry lips. "Yes, sir."

"Halloran," said Dan, "you will have

that ridge top lined with your men. When the Apaches hear Sykes's trumpeter, they should boil out of that box canyon like bees and take up position behind the rock barricade below the overhanging canyon wall. You will open fire."

Halloran tilted his head to one side. "But the major said they had perfect cover behind the rocks. What do we shoot at, sir?"

Dan waved an arm. "At the rock wall behind them. You've played billiards, Mister Halloran?"

"Yes, sir."

"Then you know how to bank your shots."

A great light dawned in Halloran's blue eyes. "The angle of rebound is the same as the angle of incidence."

Dan took off his stinking hat and bowed his head. "You're a man of quick perception, Mister Halloran."

Dan looked at Gila and Haley. "We will pull out now and go north, coming down into the canyon. When Halloran plays the open waltz we will come down the main canyon and attempt to get into the Apache camp. Our goal is to save Miss Moore and find Surgeon Cornish."

Gila whistled softly. Haley let out his breath in a soft rush.

Dan stood up. "Any questions?"

"Supposing it doesn't work?" asked Sykes.

Dan looked down at the young officer. "Why," he said, "they will close the book on Fayes' Scouts."

In the silence that followed they looked at each other. Then Sykes spoke up. "The odds are long, but I don't know where I'd rather be than here."

The canyon was already deep in shadow when Dan and his detail moved out. Riding behind him and Gila were Haley and Troopers MacDonald, Abruzzi, Schaefer, Hanson, Garrity, Delano, Black and Willis. Top shots. Rough-and-tumble boys.

None of them spoke as they picked their way through the darkness. For there are times when words make no sense, and when a man is better alone with his own secret thoughts.

Dan awoke with a start as a hard dirty hand clamped down on his working mouth. He looked up into Gila's shadowy face. The scout leaned close. "Yuh was talking loud, *amigo*."

Dan nodded. Gila withdrew his hand. The canyon was dark. A cool wind crept through the chaotic jungle of rock. Dan shivered. He looked at Gila. "What was I saying?"

Gila stowed a chew into his mouth. "Somethin' about the war. The woods. The rain."

Dan sat up and leaned back against a rock.

"One of these days you'll forget all that," said Gila.

Dan looked up at the sky. There was the faintest trace of gray light. "It's about time," he said.

"Yes."

"Awaken the men."

"Keno."

They rose up from among the rocks like a crew of dirty tramps. A rifle butt clicked and Haley cursed in fluent style. "Dammit,

Delano! You're clumsy as a cub bear!"

They sipped their stale water and chewed without appetite on their embalmed beef.

Dan stood up and tightened his gunbelt. "All right, Gila," he said.

Gila walked off through the wilderness of rocks. Dan and the men followed him. The sky was lighter now. The shoulder of rock which jutted out into the canyon loomed high above them. An eagle screamed like a file scratched across hard metal.

Fear descended upon them like a soft flying ghoul. It eased its skinny arms about Dan's neck and settled its body comfortably on his back. Each man has his own picture of fear. Dan's had somehow taken the shape of a skinny Apache, with tight parchment for skin, drawn over protruding bones, staring at him with sightless eyes. Intchi-dijn. The Black Wind.

Gila stopped at the base of the huge rock shoulder. He held up a dirty hand. They stopped silently on rawhide moccasins.

Then far away down the canyon, carried on the cold wind, came the brassy tone of the trumpet. Mister Sykes was in position.

Dan looked up at the knife-edged ridge. There was no sign of life but Halloran would be up there. His men gripping Henry rifles greasy with cold sweat, staring with strained eyes at the far wall of the big canyon.

Gila dropped to his hands and knees and crawled on, followed by Dan and the troopers. Gila stopped. "Look," he whispered.

Dan stared into the dimness. There was movement at the mouth of the box canyon. A long line of trotting Apaches, carrying their repeaters. They vanished behind the rock barricade. Minutes drifted past. Dan pictured the Apaches secure in their natural fortress, laughing at the foolish White-eyes.

It grew lighter. Now and then an Apache head popped up, to stare down the canyon and then sink down again, as though worked by a string.

Dan looked up at the ridge. "Jesus," he husked, "what's wrong?"

As though in answer he heard a faint roar of command. Then rifles sparkled along the ridge. Smoke drifted with the wind. The slugs smashed against the rock wall behind the barricade. An Apache whooped derisively. The Henry rifles on the ridge churned steadily. The echoes slammed back and forth. The whoops changed to screams. Lead pattered down behind the barricade. The two hundred and sixteen-grain slugs, driven by twenty-five grains of powder, slammed into the wall and ricocheted downward. The mutilated bullets whined through the air.

Dan stood up. "Now," he said, and took the lead, running at a crouch between the rocks.

Dan's breath came hard in his throat as he went up the rough slope. There was a feathery feeling in his lungs. This was the job for which they had been trained. The apex of the years of training and parade-ground soldiering. To shoot and be shot at.

Dan stopped behind a slab of rock. Halloran's men were emptying their fifteen-round magazines. Then the fire died away. The screams and groans of the warriors rose in a bitter crescendo. Dan went on again, glancing to his right. In the dimness behind the barricade he could see thrashing bodies and others that were still. Then he passed the mouth of the box canyon.

A young buck stood up behind a rock and looked toward the barricade. He never saw the steel-shod butt of Dan's rifle drive in to smash his skull. Dan hurled the body. Another young warrior stared at him with gaping mouth. Haley fired from the hip. The slug whirled the Tonto around. He dropped.

The canyon opened up. Wickiups showed in the dimness, like great beehives. Shadowy figures scuttled about them. The squaws hurrying their kids to safety. "Don't shoot at them unless they attack us!" yelled Dan.

"Nits breed lice!" yelled MacDonald.

"You heard the major!" shouted Haley.

Five young bucks charged Dan's party. Young men who still wore the head-scratching stick and drinking cane of the untried brave. It took guts. But guts was no defense against Henry rifle slugs fired at fifty feet. The charge was ripped apart like tissue paper and the rushing white men were through into the canyon proper.

A squaw dropped to one knee and fired a double-barreled shotgun. Both barrels flamed. Willis staggered sideways as the shot caught him in the left thigh. Then he was down, gripping the shattered limb, with gouts of blood streaming through his dirty fingers. Garrity fired twice, driving the squaw back into a hollow.

The driving crashes of Halloran's fire ripped out again. The main canyon was a hell of rifle fire and agonized screaming.

A mixed group of squaws and young warriors closed in on Dan's men. The command came automatically from Dan. "At twenty yards! Fire by squad! Aim is left oblique! *Fire!*"

Henry slugs smashed home, drove brown bodies back and down like so many bundles of clothing.

Delano went down with a thrown knife in his left shoulder. Schaefer grunted as a pistol flamed at his feet and smashed him back against a rock with half his face a bloody mask.

"There's the girl!" screamed Abruzzi.

Harriet was running up a slope pursued by a screaming squaw, whose knife-fanged claw was reaching out for the white girl's back. Gila raised his long Spencer, steadied and fired. The squaw staggered forward. The knife tip sliced through the back of Harriet's dress. She darted sideways and came on toward them.

Dan hurled a boulder. Here and there in the rocks were half-naked boys, fighting like warriors with old Burnside carbines, shotguns and bows. Dan's men dived for cover and began to pick them off one by one. A buck leaped on Garrity. Garrity came up from the ground like an uncoiling spring. His rifle barrel smashed the Tonto's skull.

Dan dropped a warrior and drew his Colt. He placed it on the rocks in front of him and began to reload his Winchester. Harriet was safe behind him. His fingers fumbled with the cartridges as he fed the magazine.

"Look!" said Gila.

The squaws had retreated with their

young ones up a narrow trail that clung like a string to the almost sheer walls. "Don't fire!" yelled Dan.

Suddenly, behind them, from the main canyon there came a roaring noise and then the smash of tons of rock. Dust billowed into the box canyon. A dozen warriors rounded the turn, full into the fire of the freshly charged Henry rifles of Dan's little command. The slugs ripped them apart, scattering them across the rocky ground.

Above the crashing of rifles came hoarse cheering from Halloran's men.

Dan crawled to Harriet. She did not speak as he slid his arm about her.

Gila ran to Dan. "Look," he said.

At the rear of the canyon a man dressed in blue was running for cover.

"Cornish," said Dan quietly.

"There's the old man," said Gila.

Black Wind was crawling up the rocks, feeling his way with clawed hands. Black raised his rifle. Dan struck it down. "Let him go," he said. "He's trapped. They both are."

Now and then a shot ripped out from the rocks as a Tonto made a last stand. The squaws were high up on the trail now.

Haley trotted up from the canyon mouth. "Halloran's fire loosened the rocks from the canyon wall. The whole goddamned mess came down on the bucks. There ain't but thirty or forty of them still alive."

Dan picked up his rifle. He looked at Harriet. "Stay here."

"Where are you going?"

Dan jerked his head. "Captain Cornish and I have a debt to settle."

"Don't go, Dan! He's mad!"

Dan picked up his Colt and slid it into his holster. He climbed over the rocks, crouched, and ran for the back of the canyon.

Dan crawled up the slope. Two hundred yards from the towering canyon wall he heard the dry voice. "Nantan Eclatten," the voice called out, "are you there?"

It was like a voice from the grave. Dan looked up. Black Wind was perched on a rock shelf above him. Behind the skinny Tonto was the mouth of a cave.

"Nantan Eclatten!"

Dan crawled closer. "I am here, Black Wind," he called out in Spanish.

The old chief nodded. "I knew it."

"Come down, old man. You are safe."

A rifle shot split the quiet.

Black Wind shook his aged head. "No. This is my last place to stay. Here I stayed for the last five years, thinking of the white man's perfidy. When the time was ripe I went back to my people."

"You have lost, Black Wind. Your warriors are all dead or captured. Your women and children have fled."

Black Wind wet his thin lips. "Yes, Nantan Eclatten. Your medicine was good. Mine was not."

Dan looked at the strange figure seated on the rocks. The wind flapped his dirty buckskin kilt. "You are safe," he said again.

Black Wind shook his head. "I will not see many grasses. I will not go to the reservation to be looked at and spoken about. I am not a child to be so treated."

"You are a great warrior, Black Wind."

"You are a greater one."

Dan looked down the slope. He could see the tall form of Denny Halloran beside Mike Haley. Halloran's men were rounding up the survivors of the *bronco* band. Sergeant French was busy with his medical panniers.

Dan looked up the slope. Myron Cornish was climbing the canyon wall. Above him there was no trail.

Dan slipped a hand into his pocket and touched the brass plate Black Wind had cast with scorn into the road at Dan's feet. "Come down," he called. "You will be treated with the honors of war."

Black Wind shook his grizzled head. "Am I only to be a number?"

"You will be treated as a great warrior."

"I once said that you should choose the way of your dying. I was wrong. It is I who will chose the way of my dying. I will die here. Along with the gods who did not smile on me in my last fight."

Dan shrugged. "As you wish." He crawled through the rocks. The canyon was light now. Cornish was high on the slope, looking down now and then with white face at the canyon below him.

Dan worked forward. Cornish opened fire at too great a range. The spent bullets spattered on the rocks.

Dan worked closer and closer until he was just below the rock wall. He left his Winchester and began to climb. His skin was ripped and abraded by the keen-edged rocks. Sweat broke out and soaked his filthy uniform.

He rested on a ledge fifty yards from Cornish.

"Fayes!" called out the surgeon, "can you hear me?"

"Yes."

"Then listen! I have thousands in gold. I'll split with you if you let me go."

"Go to hell!"

"I'll kill you if you come up here."

"We'll see."

Far down the canyon Dan could see the white faces of the troopers as they watched the two men high on the rock wall.

Cornish raised his voice. "I'll give you *all* the gold!"

"You bastard! You think you can buy your way out of this?"

Cornish began to shoot. Slugs smashed against the rocks and keened off into space.

Dan worked upward. His left leg was numbing from the strain.

Rocks fell from the ledge above him. He eased himself up on the ledge. Cornish was trying to batter a foothold in the canyon wall with his rifle butt. Dan stood up and edge behind a rock shoulder. "Cornish," he called out, "drop that gun!"

Cornish turned. He threw it down and jerked a pistol from his belt. His thin lips worked as he looked at Dan. "You spoiled the sweetest plan a man ever made up," he said.

Dan cocked the Colt. "Throw down that gun, Cornish!"

Cornish fired. The slug whipped past Dan. Dan snatched his hat free from his head with his left hand and scaled it at Cornish's face. Cornish automatically threw up his left hand to guard his face. Dan fired. The big Colt kicked back hard into his hand. Dust puffed from the dusty blouse.

Cornish took two steps forward and then swayed toward the lip of the ledge. His eyes were glazing even as he fired. The slug picked at Dan's left shoulder like a burning iron and then Cornish went over the ledge. He screamed once as he turned head over heels and struck with a sickening smash far below.

Dan walked to the edge of the ledge and looked down. The dead man's head was twisted hard to one side. Blood flowed from the slack mouth.

Dan holstered his Colt and started down.

Harriet came to meet him. The sun had tipped the canyon rim, shining down on sprawled bodies and empty wickiups; on empty cartridge cases and bloody knives.

Halloran grinned as he saw Dan. "You've written a new page in the book," he said.

Harriet rested her head on Dan's shoulder.

Gila looked up at Black Wind. "What about him?" he asked.

"Let him be."

As though in answer Black Wind raised his cracked voice. "Nantan Eclatten!" he called.

Dan turned.

The old chief raised his skinny arms. *"Dih asd-za hig-e balgon-ya-hi dont-e shilg-nli-dah!"* he intoned.

Gila shifted his chew. "This I have done and what has come about is all the same to me!" he translated.

The command was silent as they looked at the old man.

"The last of the rimrock *broncos*," said Dan.

Gila nodded. "One of the greatest. Yuh know somethin', Dan? I got a lot of respect for that old bastard."

The scouts moved out at noon leaving a plume of smoke rising from the burning wickiups. The blue-faced dead were buried in a rock cleft, troopers and Tontos alike. Dan looked back as they reached the canyon mouth. The old man had toppled sideways against the side of the shallow cave.

High above him a buzzard floated on the still hot air, drifting through the veil of smoke, patiently awaiting his time for the feast.

"He won't get much," said Gila dryly.

Down the canyon Trumpeter Criswell lipped into Assembly, bouncing the brazen notes of the C trumpet from the ancient rock walls. The troopers rode loose and easy in their saddles.

Dan looked at Harriet. She smiled through the dust. He held out a hand and gripped hers.

The Tontos were broken but the Chiricahuas still held their mountain fastnesses to the south. There was a long trail ahead of any soldier in Arizona Territory. But soldiering was a way of life to which he was dedicated. A hard life without monetary award. But his command had been blooded properly now. The long years of his near disgrace had been burned out in the hell of canyons and chattering rifle fire. He had squared his account.

Dan looked back at the wreathing smoke

drifting high above the canyon. "*Yadalanh*, Intchi-dijn," he said quietly. "Farewell, Black Wind!"

THE END

Books by Gordon D. Shirreffs in the Linford Western Library:

THE VALIANT BUGLES
SHOWDOWN IN SONORA
SOUTHWEST DRIFTER
SHADOW VALLEY
TOP GUN
AMBUSH ON THE MESA
BUGLES ON THE PRAIRIE
FORT VENGEANCE

Other titles in the Linford Western Library:

FARGO: MASSACRE RIVER
by John Benteen

Fargo spurred his horse to the edge of the road. Its right hind hoof slipped perilously over the edge as he forced it around the wagon. Ahead he saw Jade Ching riding hard, bent low in her saddle. Fargo rammed home his spurs and drove his mount up to her. The ambushers up ahead had now blocked the road. Fargo's convoy was a jumble, a perfect target for the insurgents' weapons!

SUNDANCE: DEATH IN THE LAVA
by John Benteen

The land echoed with the thundering hoofs of Modoc ponies. In minutes they swooped down and captured the wagon train and its cargo of gold. But now the halfbreed they called Sundance was going after it, and he swore nothing would stand in his way—not Indian savagery of the vicious gunfighters of the town named Hell.

FARGO: THE SHARPSHOOTERS
by John Benteen

The Canfield clan, thirty strong, were raising hell in Texas. One of them had shot a Texas Ranger, and the Rangers had to bring in the killer. The last thing they wanted though was a feud. Fargo, arrested for gunrunning, was promised he could go free if he would walk into the Canfield's lair and bring out the killer. And Fargo was tough enough to hold his own against the whole clan.

SUNDANCE: OVERKILL
by John Benteen

Sundance's reputation as a fighting man had spread from Canada to Mexico, from the Mississippi to the Pacific. There was no job too tough for the halfbreed to handle. So when a wealthy banker's daughter was kidnapped by the Cheyenne, he offered Sundance $10,000 to rescue the girl. Sundance became a moving target for both the U.S. Cavalry and his own blood brothers.

DAY OF THE COMANCHEROS
by Steven C. Lawrence

Their very name struck terror into men's hearts—the Comancheros, a savage army of cutthroats who swept across Texas, leaving behind a bloodstained trail of robbery and murder. When Tom Slattery stumbled on some of their slaughtered victims, he found only one survivor, young Anna Peterson. With a cavalry escort, he set out to bring the murderers to justice.

SUNDANCE: SILENT ENEMY
by John Benteen

Both the Indians and the U.S. Cavalry were being victimized. A lone crazed Cheyenne was on a personal war path against both sides and neither brigades of bluecoats nor tribes of braves could end his reign of terror. They needed to pit one man against one crazed Indian. That man was Sundance.

GUNS OF FURY
by Ernest Haycox

Dane Starr, alias Dan Smith, wanted to close the door on his past and hang up his guns, but people wouldn't let him. Good men wanted him to settle their scores for them. Bad men thought they were faster and itched to prove it. Starr had to keep killing just to stay alive.

FARGO: PANAMA GOLD
by John Benteen

A soldier of fortune named Cleve Buckner was recruiting an army of killers, gunmen and deserters from all over Central America. With foreign money behind him, Buckner was going to destroy the Panama Canal before it could be completed. Fargo's job was to stop Buckner—and to eliminate him once and for all!

HELL RIDERS

by Steve Mensing

Outlaw Wade Walker's kid brother, Duane, was locked up in the Silver City jail facing a rope at dawn. When Wade rode into town the sheriff knew trouble had already begun. Wade was a ruthless outlaw, but he was smart, and he had vowed to have his brother out of jail before morning!

DESERT OF THE DAMNED

by Nelson Nye

The law was after him for the murder of a marshal—a murder he didn't commit. Breen was after him for revenge—and Breen wouldn't stop at anything . . . blackmail, a frameup . . . or murder. He was desperate now and vowed to find a way out—or make one.

LASSITER

by Jack Slade

Lassiter wasn't the kind of man to listen to reason. Cross him once and he'd hold a grudge for years to come—if he let you live that long. But he was no crueler than the men he had killed, and he had never killed a man who didn't need killing.

LAST STAGE TO GOMORRAH

by Barry Cord

Jeff Carter, tough ex-riverboat gambler, now had himself a horse ranch that kept him free from gunfights and card games. Until Sturvesant of Wells Fargo showed up. Jeff owed him a favour and Sturvesant wanted it paid up. All he had to do was to go to Gomorrah, a one-time boom town, and recover a quarter of a million dollars stolen from a stagecoach!

McALLISTER ON THE COMANCHE CROSSING

by Matt Chisholm

The Comanche, deadly warriors and the finest horsemen in the world, reckon McAllister owes them a life—and the trail is soaked with the blood of the men who had tried to outrun them before.

QUICK-TRIGGER COUNTRY

by Clem Colt

Turkey Red hooked up with Curly Bill Graham's outlaw crew and soon made a name for himself. But wholesale murder was out of Turk's line, so when range war flared he bucked the whole border gang alone . . .

PISTOL LAW

by Paul Evan Lehman

Lance Jones came back to Mustang for just one thing—Revenge! Revenge on the people who had him thrown in jail; on the crooked marshal; on the human vulture who had already taken over the town. Now it was Lance's turn . . .